SPIDERS IN THE GRAVEYARD

SPIDERS OF SPY BOOK TWO

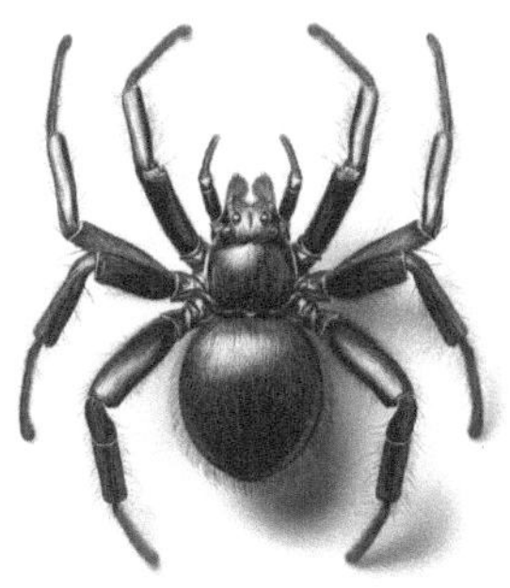

MAX THORNTON

As the author of the Max Thornton books, I thoroughly
enjoyed writing *Hardly a Challenge*, which led to the
Spider books, along with the stand-alone *The Silent
Slaughters*, *Red Dust* and *Barbed Wire*, yet to be published.
Each have real life lessons slotted in as part of their stories,
reminding the reader that life can bare its teeth without notice.
For those who have bought and read my books, thank you.
Books are the avenue to developing the mind and helping you
to understand the world around you. Reading a book gives you
extra knowledge, and lessons in life. And may a long reading
life be given to you all.

Note: The author has chosen Max Thornton as his pen name
for his journey through life and when writing exciting fiction
novels. It bears no resemblance to any other person who may
have the same name.

With the exception of those who have given permission
to use their names, the names of people and places have
been purposely changed or deleted.

This book is for my wife, Penny.

Our tomorrows still hold unspoken stories.

There is no more sincere love
than my evergreen love for you.

Prologue

Spider, spider on the wall,
How is it you never fall?

I t was 5 January 2010, and winter had set itself in. A blanket of snow had settled down over most of London, which was really not unusual for this time of year. While tourists and those with nothing to do admired the soft and silent descending snow, this was not the case for Stewart MacGregor.

Stewart was shaving snow off the front entrance paths to the old convent school with a snow shovel, a job he would have to do more than once. He was a Scotsman through and through, a strong man who would be sixty this year, and the caretaker and maintenance man at St Agnes Catholic Finishing School for Girls, housed in an old convent in the Chiltern Hills. He also drove and maintained the thirty-seater St Agnes bus.

It was hard to believe this lovely sleepy centuries-old town surrounded by green rolling hills was only a ninety-minute drive from London. St Agnes' fourteenth-century church and stone buildings which surrounded the graveyard in Hambleden in Buckinghamshire were all within a cobblestoned, fenced area. The majestic oak doors of the church in their natural grain colours, obviously had the ability to withstand the harsh weather over centuries while still maintaining their appearance and charm .

The school was run by four nuns and a Mother Superior. Young girls aged fourteen to eighteen had been sent here by their well-to-do parents since the 1800s. Each year, twenty-four young girls would study a very strict curriculum. They would be taught the finer details of a lady of society and substance, one of the prerequisites of enrolment being a fluent use of the French language.

Nuns had been placed here over more than a hundred years and were usually replaced after five years. None of the four current hard-nosed nuns had any tolerance for young girl's tantrums, jocularity or frivolous behaviour.

The most reverent Father O'Reilly was the local priest who performed Sunday Mass and Holy Communion. He had nothing to do with the girls school and had been reminded of that on many occasions by the nuns who were very protective of their territorial boundaries.

In two weeks' time, twenty-four young girls would arrive and be subjected to a year of life they could never have imagined.

Chapter One

Hanna lived on the Gold Coast in Queensland, Australia. She was from a wealthy family whose parents owned sixty per cent of shares in a large car company importing from India and Japan. She was being groomed for a position on the board of management. She had just completed a term at a business college and was getting her things together for London.

Prior to her term at business college, she had spent the previous two years at a very expensive ladies boarding college in Switzerland, where she and a girl named Rosanna had become lifelong friends. Rosanna's parents were also wealthy. Her father was the heir to the family's lucrative diamond mine in Africa, owned and operated by the family, that had been sending diamonds around the world for more than one hundred years. Rosanna had been brought up among diamond conversations her whole life. She knew everything there was to know about diamonds. She knew they were the hardest natural substance known to man, and that they were fifty-eight times harder than the next hardest mineral on earth. The only substance that could scratch a diamond was another diamond, and a diamond over one carat in weight was one in a million. She lived in the chic Parisian suburb of Neuilly-sur-Seine. Rosanna was also being groomed for a position in the family business, and as such was also attending the school at St Agnes.

Rosanna and Hanna were both eighteen years old. The two girls were over the moon when they learned they would be reunited again.

*

St Agnes' boarding facilities were old but well-kept and stylish in what could only be explained as medieval architecture, due to the small corridors, winding spiral staircases and the dark stained colour of every wall and timber structure. For the most part, even though the rooms were dark and gloomy, up high were large cathedral windows that let the morning sun in and allowed the afternoon shadows to dance among the timber structures. Upstairs were six rooms, four beds in each, with four wardrobes and bedside tables. There were no ensuites in the rooms; the communal bathroom and toilets, while clean, were old, with rows of open showers and toilets admitting no privacy.

The dining room and training rooms were downstairs. The front entrance had a gate house that reminded everyone of Gothic architecture. Behind the large magnificent oak double doors that had survived the test of time was the front entrance and the great hall with signs of yesteryear meetings and community discussions, with a large, cold kitchen where the nuns would take turns at preparing the meals. The small chapel was in the centre of the building, where evening prayer would be held. On Sundays they would all attend the main church.

Everywhere you looked were signs that said, 'Unless you are spoken to, or you have something important to say, do not speak', a reminder of the strict rules to be adhered to within the Catholic society convents of earlier days, which looked like they had been carried forward here.

Chapter Two

The girls arrived in dribs and drabs and were directed to their rooms. Rosanna and Hanna walked in together to make sure they were put in the same room. There were two girls already there, Clara and Edith, both only fourteen years old. Clara was a scrawny little thing with her hair done in plaits. Edith was the opposite, not fat but chubby. She was obviously of the opinion that it didn't matter how much you ate, your earrings would always fit. She was a nonstop talker; she obviously had not seen the signs yet, but she would soon get the message.

Hanna said, 'Have you looked at this place, Rosie? It's bursting at the seams with secrets and untold stories, and it's looking for a voice to tell the long-hidden truths of sadness, love and the dark times of days gone by, hidden and long forgotten with the passing of time. You could transport someone back here from the past and this place would still be familiar.'

When they had all arrived, they were summoned to the great hall for the official welcome and introductions. The maintenance man, Stewart, was introduced. The girls were told they were not to go to him directly; they were to go through one of the nuns, which caused some sniggering among the girls. The Mother Superior introduced the four nuns.

'This is Sister Mary. She will be in charge of etiquette, dining and table manners. You will only communicate with her in French. Sister Theresa will be teaching how to walk and sit like a lady with practising to walk and sit like royalty. Sister Claudine will be in charge of sport and morning exercises. And last but not least is Sister Ignatius who is in charge of discipline.

'We will keep it simple for the first couple of days. A roster will be placed on the noticeboard in the great hall listing the day-to-day jobs and the girls' names allocated to those jobs. There will also be a list of names of the girls that will pull the belltower ropes on Sunday. The belltower has eight bells and will be rung for thirty minutes before the main service. The bells will also ring for weddings and funerals, but that will not be your responsibility. There will be four internal bells throughout the day. When you hear the first at 6 am, you will rise and complete your jobs, exercise in the yard, shower and dress. The second bell will be breakfast at 7.30 am, and latecomers will not be permitted in the dining room. The third bell will be lunch at 12.30 pm; again, no latecomers permitted in the dining room. And the fourth bell will be the evening meal at 6 pm; again, no latecomers. At 7.30 pm, organ music will play, and the chapel doors will open for prayer or silent meditation for fifteen minutes; everyone will attend. Eight pm till lights out at nine-thirty is for your own personal hygiene, washing and or ironing.

'While you are here, you will know doubt hear all sorts of rumours and stories of buried treasures from the past. They are just that – rumours. So, I will save you the trouble of having to listen to them all by telling you of what I know, some of which is fact. The River Thames was the main supply route for more than fifty per cent of supplies and human trade to England. Ships carrying sugar and rum from the West Indies, tea and spices from the East Indies, wine from the Mediterranean, furs, timber and hemp from Russia, gold and salt, sugar and cotton and enslaved people from Africa, tobacco, lumber, rice, and dried fish from America – the Thames was a beehive of ships and boat activity in the 1700s. There were no docks built along the river for the large vessels to unload. Small sailing barges were used to unload the ships and take the supplies to the shore where horse-drawn carts were waiting. These barges took up some of the space on the river that the bigger vessels were jostling for.

'Also sailing up the river from the North Sea in the 1700s was a famous pirate named Calico Jack. He had in his crew two female cutthroat pirates, Anne Bonny and Mary Read. It is rumoured that among the many treasures he had stolen from merchant foreign vessels were the Tongzhi Emperor's Zhonghu Chengzhi coins minted during the Qing Dynasty in China, with a valuation of around ten million pounds. It is also rumoured that among his ill-gotten gains were double leopard gold coins, issued for a period of only six months in July 1344, England's rarest medieval coin. He also had more than two hundred silver pennies and last but by no means least, a solid golden eagle that had come from Egypt hundreds of years ago. It is priceless. It has an inscription underneath that says, "The bearer will witness or suffer no pain, but this eagle must be shared again and again". Pirates were very superstitious, so they shared it from ship to ship until it suddenly disappeared in the seventeenth century, and it has never been seen again. The historical nutters will tell you the eagle came here among Calico Jack's treasure. However, there is no positive proof that this is true, just another rumour to keep people guessing.

'It is also rumoured that, prior to his capture in 1700, he and the two female pirates rowed ashore somewhere near here in Hambleden with the treasures in steel containers. They were either buried or hidden away to be collected at a later date. However, Calico Jack was caught and sentenced to death in Port Royal in Jamaica, his body put on display, and he must have been buried there. Bonny and Read were both pregnant, so their deaths were delayed. Read died of the fever during her sentence and would have been buried alongside Calico Jack. Bonny disappeared and was never seen again. Once again, it is rumoured she was seen praying here in the St Agnes Church sometime later, which of course sparked the rumours that the treasure must have been close by for her to have been here.

Now, let's not hear any more about treasures!'

'Jesus,' said Hanna later in their room, 'how are we going to survive this crap for a whole year? Can't see it happening.'

Rosie said, 'Yep, we've been shoved into a convent living with a bunch of nutters.'

Clara and Edith were on the verge of tears.

Don't worry, kids,' said Hanna, 'we will deal with it and come up with a plan of our own.'

Chapter Three

Hambleden boasted a population of about eight hundred residents. This unspoiled charming village fitted perfectly into its surrounds. The cottages were made of brick and flint and the roofs were topped with red tiles. They had flower boxes at the dormer windows and perfectly trimmed flower gardens behind white picket fences. The village had a store-cum-post office where any more than two people in the post office was considered a crowd. There was also a shop and cafe, a bakery, a Wheelers Family butcher shop, a pub and a working waterwheel flour mill that used to provided flour for the town residents and surrounding villages. The flour mill and waterwheel were a mile south of the town at Mill End on the Thames.

The nearest police station was at Beaconsfield, half an hour away, with a sergeant and four police officers, a military style Land Rover, a motorbike and two pushbikes. There was also a police station at Marlow, four miles away.

Stewart had gone home at the end of the day to find two men waiting outside his cottage. One of the men, a tall man in his forties, said his name was Joran. He was dressed immaculately in a sandy coloured suit with a neat blue tie, a short back and sides haircut, and had an unmistakable Australian accent. It wasn't the suit or the tie that concerned Stewart; it was the bulge in the jacket.

The other person was little Paddy O'Flarity who was the graveyard caretaker and gravedigger. He had on his blue bib and brace overalls inscribed with "Paddy, Hambleden Parish Council". He had bowed legs, strong calcified hands and red hair. You could tell before he opened his mouth that he was Irish.

Joran said he was a private historian contracted by a book company called The Whole Story, who were writing a book on the area, and particularly the graveyard, the church and the waterwheel mill on the banks of the river at Mill End.

'What is it you expect from us?' said Stewart.

'Well, I would like to be able to wander around without creating suspicion amongst the residents.'

'We can't give you that', said Paddy. 'You will need the parish council's approval. They will sit this Wednesday at 7 pm. You will need to notify them you wish to attend.'

Stewart said, 'And you will need approval from the church verger . His name is Allen, but everyone calls him AJ. I will give you his contact details.'

Joran said, 'I didn't think it would become so involved.'

They reminded him he would be walking among objects and artefacts dating back to 1400, and graves in the graveyard dating back to the twelfth century, and if he wanted access, he would need the proper authority.

'The graveyard is split into two areas,' said Paddy, 'pre- and post-1906. There is a map in the church vestry for post-1906 but there are no details recorded prior to that. You would have to find those graves yourself, or whatever it is you're looking for.'

After Joran had gone, Stewart said, 'He's no more an historian than the pope is a monk. And did you see he was carrying a gun? What does an historian researcher need a gun for?'

Paddy said, 'He might be scared a boogeyman might jump out of a grave and grab him. Nevertheless, I think we should include the police in all of this. We'll ask Sergeant John Weir to meet us in the Stag and Huntsman pub later tonight if he can.'

'It's all very bloody suspicious, if you ask me,' said Stewart.

Chapter Four

The first bell rang at 6 am but most of the girls were not at the morning exercises with Sister Claudine. She wasn't surprised. It usually happened on the first day, but tomorrow would see all twenty-four girls at the morning exercises.

They showered and dressed. Those who weren't at the exercises were made to stand outside the dining room and wait. There would be no breakfast for those that weren't there that day. Most of the girls were sent back to change into the uniforms that had been placed on their bed the night before. Short skirts and flimsy see-through tops were never going to cut it.

The girls were divided into groups and sent to their various classes. The classes were in four groups of six, and Rosie and Hanna made sure that they were in a permanent group with Edith and Clara. They could hear the other group in Sister Mary's classroom babbling away in French. Their group was with Sister Theresa all day today, walking, sitting, leg and skirt positions, standing, turning, bending and squatting. Their uniforms were designed for their training. Skirts were just below the knees and the blouses had the correct number of buttons undone at the top. The shorts and singlets for morning exercises were short enough to enable free movement but not short enough to expose female anatomy. Socks were white and sandshoes were canvas that needed whitening each day.

There was a white line on the floor in the classroom that they walked along with books on their head. It was done to encourage them to stand with a straight back and a long neck with eyes looking forward. Even when they thought they were doing it right, the books fell off their heads.

Rosie said, 'We are all getting a sore neck, Sister.'

They moved on to sitting with legs crossed and legs placed sideways with the skirt always in the right position. Sister Theresa turned out to be one of the best with a small sense of humour and a secret flirt. She told them on the quiet that if they wanted to attract a small amount of attention, they could move the skirt up slightly higher.

'But you didn't hear that from me,' she said with a smile and a wink.

The bell rang for lunch, and no one was late. Lunch consisted of cold spam, chopped pork and ham sandwiches and bottles of cordial with throwaway cups.

Hanna said, 'I can't wait to see what's for dinner.'

The third group was the lucky ones today as they were playing basketball with Sister Claudine. The fourth group was being lectured by Sister Ignatius on disciplinary measures when it came to fraternising with the male counterpart, sexual relationships and the importance of being on time for meetings or organised functions.

'This nonsense about the bride being late is rubbish, invented by some upstart woman and her mother. There is nothing nice or good about being late. Punctuality is the sign of a professional, organised woman, and don't you forget it, young ladies!'

While they were in their classes, the clothes they were to wear to the evening meal had been placed on their beds. (All the clothes they were given were exactly the right sizes, as their measurements had been sent ahead of their arrival.) Long skirts, heeled shoes, a plain white top with quarter-length sleeves and a knitted scarf in the colour of their group; Rosie and Hanna's group was buttercup yellow. They were allowed one piece of jewellery; some chose earrings or a necklace. Rosie and Hanna chose a ring given to each of them by their secret admirers when they had left.

What they didn't know was the nuns said grace for breakfast and lunch, but one of the girls would be called upon to say grace at the evening meals. And the nuns expected a bit more than the usual 'what we are about to receive' job. Rosie, Hanna, Edith and Clara sat together, closed their eyes and crossed their fingers. None of them were chosen.

'Thank goodness it's not us,' they said. 'We will write one down and bring it with us and we can all use it if we have to.'

Dinner was an extravaganza of cold meat and salad with rich, thick, creamy sago pudding for dessert. After dinner, their time was their own but there was so much to do before the next day, and most times they needed to help Edith and Clara to get things done. In the morning, if they had finished their jobs, they would find each other and help.

That was the beginning of playing the system with its own rules, and there would be more of that to come. Rosie and Hanna had been around a bit longer than most and had a few more moves up their sleeve, like finding a safe place for a late-night fag.

Chapter Five

Paddy, Stewart and Sergeant Weir were in the Stag and Huntsman consuming a pint of Guinness and discussing the issue of whom they considered to be the mystery man calling himself Joran. They explained to Sergeant Weir, whom they had known long enough to call Johno, that this bloke was in no way a historian, and he was carrying a concealed weapon.

'When you rang me,' said Johno, 'I checked his name, and he has a licence to carry a weapon. I don't know why; the permit doesn't say. In fact, if you want more information about him, his name comes to a dead end – very strange. I tried to go a bit higher in the system and was virtually told to "go away, it's above your pay grade. Be very careful how you deal with him." They said they didn't want to antagonise the issue, so for now you will get no help, whatever that means.'

'Jesus, begod,' said Paddy, 'what's the next move now then? I think we need some help to deal with this.'

'Well,' said Johno, 'when you pray for rain, you have to deal with the mud. I think we should just go along with who he said he is, give him his authority to poke around and play it from there. But tomorrow I will introduce myself and offer him any assistance the police can give him. If nothing else, that will send him back to the drawing board on how he will go about whatever he is here for.'

The police arranged for the parish council and the church rector to all be at the meeting on the Wednesday night. The parish council was made up of the older members of the town, who like most small town council members, were of the opinion that nothing could happen in their town unless they gave the approval. Sergeant Weir jokingly said they were only one step away from the police having to report to them.

Johno, Paddy and Stewart were also there, as they would become part of whatever was going on. Sergeant Weir said he had welcomed Joran to the area and offered the police support if he needed it, and that they would be taking an interest in what he was doing there.

After some deliberation with some of the parish councillors, who were not happy, approval was given with some constraints. The graves were not to be tampered with, and the old crypts were not to be entered or broken into. St Agnes Girls College was out of bounds, other than that they gave him permission to move around the church and the graveyard. The owners of the waterwheel mill were happy for him to look around provided they got a mention in the book he was supposed to be working on.

*

It wasn't long before three phone calls were made from an unknown location in London, which led to two men and a woman being dispatched to Hambleden. They were known killer operatives contracted by The Syndicate, a worldwide group of evil people from all walks of life. They had connections for hire all over the world, from the highest places down to the lowest scumbags. Those types in the lower system were considered expendable cannon fodder and were used as just that. Most of The Syndicate's field operatives had their own nicknames.

Three Fingers and his gun moll Dolly were sent when the cover of husband and wife were needed; however, they were the most unlikely married couple you could imagine. She had no idea of how to dress like a middle class married woman, with her jubblies hanging out the top of her blouse, short skirts leaving nothing for the imagination, too much make-up and lipstick along with black laced stockings and six-inch stiletto shoes. He wore a pinstriped suit, black and white saddle shoes and brogues, a bow tie and a felt fedora hat or a homburg. Dolly kept a small revolver in her bra; Three Fingers kept his .38 Special revolver in a shoulder holster. The other operative was known as Tick Tock; he was a time bomb expert and very experienced with explosives, but his gun was telling everyone it was stuck in the back of his pants.

They were on their way to Hambleden.

Chapter Six

n Australia, on Friday 5 February 2010, it was hot and humid. The Spiders were arriving at Fairview, Max and Jane's place at Lakes Entrance, for their usual quarterly weekend barbecue and get-together.

The Spiders only used their code names if they had to talk on a secure radio link with the Australian Secret Intelligence Service (ASIS). When they did, these were the nicknames they used. Joe (Slim) and Lois, (Slowpoke), Bruce (Brewster) and Sue (Auntie), Max (Wiggy) and Jane (Tuppence), and Lieutenant Commander Harrigan, who had become a friend of the Spiders after their last mission.

Joe had sold his trike; Lois's hairdresser bills had taken its toll on finance, so the trike had to go. He had now bought one of those Japanese Isuzu things. Maria and Nitro wouldn't be coming as she was not well; she had developed internal problems from being stabbed in Europe on a mission two years ago. Brian had retired from the military police and was overseas on holiday with his wife, Emma. The rest were all there for the weekend, overcooking the steak and burning the prawns. Having scraped the barbecue plate with the shovel, they all settled down in the deck chairs on the lawn overlooking the ocean, sipping a $120 bottle of Penfolds Bin 389 Cabernet Sauvignon Shiraz.

Max said, 'So, what's going on in the big bad world these days, Commander?'

'I'm not up to speed with everything these days, but there is something brewing in a small sleepy town outside London called Hambleden on the River Thames. There is a very expensive Catholic girls finishing school there that has been operating since the 1800s in an old convent, and although the building is hundreds of years old, it's a bit more upmarket these days. Whether that has anything to do with it, I don't know.'

'Sounds interesting,' said Joe. 'Can you get more information?'

'Jesus,' Max said, 'you're not thinking what I'm thinking you're thinking, are you?'

'Well, it would be interesting to just follow what's happening over there. Give us something to do here, watching what unfolds.'

'Yeah, bullshit!' said Max. 'I know you. Eventually that won't be good enough for you and we'll all be packing a bag.'

'No, we won't,' said Lois. 'We're not going anywhere, so keep out of it, Joe!'

He smiled and winked at Max, and Max knew exactly what that meant.

The Commander said, 'The history of Hambleden is full of rumours of pirate's gold and silver treasures from the 1400s to the 1700s, secret passageways under fourteenth-century churches and crypts that hold bodies of infamous outlaws, pirates and slaves, and who knows what else came down the river Thames in those days to be buried and forgotten in time.'

'Now you're getting me interested,' said Max.

'You know our motto,' said Jane, 'One in, all in – and we're not going.'

The Commander watched all this bantering going on with his friends and couldn't help smiling. He reckoned he knew what the final outcome would be, although they were now two years older than they were when they were last active. Max was now eighty-two and the others seventy-two and up. But you couldn't put anything past these old Spiders, and they were very fit. So, who knew what they would do if they treated it as just a treasure hunt with no danger to be had? It might be just what they needed.

Chapter Seven

The Syndicate operatives had arrived in Hambleden in a hired Land Rover and had split up. Three Fingers and Dolly were staying at the Stag and Huntsman and Tick Tock was staying at the Hambleden Manor bed and breakfast. He "introduced" himself to Three Fingers and Dolly at the pub that night, pretending not to know each other for the benefit of the locals who would be curious about the strangers in town.

Their mission was to ascertain if anyone else was in town looking for the Calico treasure, and if so, check on their progress, get any useful information from them, and once the treasure was found, dispose of them. The treasure was then to be handed over to a Syndicate member at a place to be advised at a later date.

The three of them arrived the next day at the graveyard gates with pen and paper on a clipboard and a camera. They were met by Paddy who saw them coming.

He said, 'Good morning to you all. I'm the graveyard caretaker. Can I be of any help?'

'No, thanks. We are just taking some notes and pictures for a book we are writing.'

Paddy thought to himself, *They are no more writing a book*

than I am sleeping with Marilyn Monroe. The bloke in the pinstripe suit was carrying a gun. She was no more his wife than one of the women in the grave was; she looked more like a prostitute. And the bloke they called Tick Tock had a permanent, sickly smirk on his face, with three-quarter-length hair, a real bad egg.

Paddy said, 'A lot of people suddenly writing books here.'

'Oh, who would that be?' they said.

'Someone calling himself Joran, staying at the Riverside Inn at Marlow four miles from here.'

'Thanks,' they said, before going into the cemetery.

Paddy left the graveyard to look for Stewart who was cutting the hedge at the girls' college.

'You'd better come down here and listen to this,' Paddy said. 'Three bad-looking people, one a woman, were at the graveyard just now. Said they were writing a book. Bullshit, of course. The one who called himself Three Fingers was carrying a gun, said the woman was his wife – more bullshit. She looked and dressed like a prostitute; she was probably his moll. We need to talk to Johno again. There is something big going down here, mate, and I don't think it's going to be good for any of us.'

Sergeant Weir sent two bobbies to check out the new arrivals. They checked their passports, later revealed to be fake. They let that slide as it was more important to leave them alone to find out why they were here.

*

After their interview with the police of this sleepy hollow, whom they thought they had fooled, the goons were at the town hall, checking old street maps where sewer drains went and any other underground information they could find.

A voice nearby said to the town clerk, 'Where are the journals from the fourteenth and seventeenth centuries?'

She said, 'Oh, hello, Joran. They are down in aisle fourteen, top shelf.'

As he headed that way, Dolly said, 'Did you see that? That's him, the other one looking for the treasure. Now we know what he looks like, and he won't be a pushover. We will bide our time and see what he knows.'

Joran found the journal he wanted, and there at the bottom of a page marked 1700 to 1800 was this:

Last Will and Testimony of John Rackham, "Calico Jack",
18 November 1720, Port Royal

Today I meet the hangman, the last person I will ever see,
so, I leave these words for someone much smarter than me.
The wheel of time waits for no man or beast,
just like the old man patiently making bread from his flour
and yeast.
I watched the birds riding the wheel to get wet,
and the kids at the bottom catching fish in a net.
The paddles reach the top and get dried in the sun,
as I sat there and watched with my bottle of rum.
One never knows the stories that old wheels been told,
or the secrets the wheel could possibly hold.
So, God bless England and a death wish for the Governor.

Remarkably interesting, Joran said to himself, but that was not what he was looking for. On the next page, he found what he wanted: Britain's trade period, 1700 through to the twentieth century, by way of the Thames, and in particular supplies, human trade and diamonds from Africa. He took copies of the thirty pages that pertained to the history he had been sent for.

Chapter Eight

The young ladies, as they were now being called, had grudgingly conformed to the strict routine and actually looked forward to seeing what clothes had been laid out for them each evening for dinner. Someone had a wonderful eye for young women's modest fashion clothing, and in keeping with what a professional and tasteful woman would wear and at dinner. They admired each other's clothes. It hadn't struck them yet, but they were becoming beautiful, young, groomed women at the hands of experts in women's social and public behaviour in their dress and bearing.

They were told that they would be taken for their first practical test at the Manor House dining room. They would be sitting in a group of four: two young men and two young ladies. The boys would be coming from a private boy's school in London. They would be closely supervised during the meal for table manners, conversation and the clothes they chose to wear, and they would be marked accordingly towards their end of year results. A similar practical public appearance would take place near the end of the year in London.

At the dinner at the Manor House, Hanna wore an off-the-shoulder navy maxi gown with sheer sleeves, matching clutch bag and shoes. Rosie, who would be at the same table, wore an emerald green, embroidered maxi dress with flared sleeves, and matching shoes and bag. She said, 'Let's go tease a boy.'

The tables were covered in white cloth and set for four people. The cutlery settings were, as they were taught, from the left: a bread plate, a salad and dinner fork, a dinner plate, and a dinner knife and soup spoon. A desert fork and spoon were at the top of the dinner plate with a water and wine glass angled to the right.

The boys had obviously been taught some form of etiquette, as they stood when the girls arrived and held the chair for them to sit, and when the girls excused themselves to go to the powder room, the boys stood when they left and again when they came back. An Australian boy, Graeme Gawman, was the least formal, the most relaxed and the most talkative. He managed to relax the rest of them at the table, especially when he whispered that he thought the present government was a shower of shit.

While they were in the powder room having a quick fag, Hanna said she thought the boys were being observed and marked as well as they were on their best behaviour.

Sister Mary came back from the powder room and said, 'Someone's been smoking in the lady's room. Our college is a smoke-free college and will remain so. Any future occurrence and the offender will be sent home.'

Rosie and Hanna looked at each other. The boys looked at them and knew that it was they who had been smoking.

Graeme said, 'Shit, that's a bit harsh. I think they're going to search your bags. If we get searched, it's not so bad. Pass the fags under the table and we will take them with us.'

They did and, yes the girl's bags were searched. After the dinner, the girls thanked them for saving their skin.

'You're welcome,' they said. 'Good luck and take care.'

Chapter Nine

Three Fingers, Dolly and Tick Tock had been in the graveyard for the last hour with the only map that was available, which was of no value to them. They were only interested in graves and headstones from 1400 to 1800, and there were many from that era. Most of the early graves were high on the hill of the graveyard and were now just a piece of stone stuck in the dirt at all angles, battered and broken from hundreds of years of storms and harsh weather, the names, ages and dates almost impossible to read. Some were just broken stone lying on the ground.

They were looking for the graves of John Rackham (Calico Jack's real name), Anne Bonny and Mary Read. If they weren't buried here, where were they? Later, the locals at the pub told them that Calico Jack had been hanged at Port Royal and he was buried there along with Mary Read. If they wanted to find their graves, they would be going to Port Royal in Jamaica. But who knew where Anne Bonny was buried? She had disappeared but was rumoured to have returned there. So, she could be buried there somewhere, but the task to find her unmarked grave would be difficult.

Joran had been in the town for a little bit longer than Three

Fingers and his cohorts, so the town folk at the pub knew him. When he came in for a drink, he was invited to join a group of locals at their table.

'Hello, Joran. Do you know who those unsavoury looking people are over there?'

He looked over at them. One of them smiled at him, or was it a slimy smirk?

'No,' he said, 'but the police told me they were here to gather information for a book.'

'Yeah, bullshit,' said the town clerk. 'Look at them. I'll guarantee you they never went past the fourth grade.'

'How do you know I'm not here for what I've told everyone?'

'You, my friend,' said the lady from the waterwheel mill, 'have been checked and passed by the police. And I'm quite sure that Sergeant Weir would be right on to them, whatever they're up to.'

On his way out, Dolly called out, 'Hey, big boy! We would like you to join us for a drink.'

Joran thought, *Well, it's one way to find out who they are,* so he said, 'Okay, no worries.'

Dolly made sure he sat next to her. As he sat down, he could see down her revealing top and unusual shape in her bra next to her breast, and he knew it wasn't part of her anatomy.

'Well, what brings someone like you to Sleepy Hollow?' she said.

'Who is someone like me? he replied.

'An upstanding clean-shaven professional businessman like you could not possibly have a business interest in the back blocks of England,' she said.

'I could own this whole town for all you know, so don't be

so quick to make a judgement. It could prove to be fatal on your part.'

He watched as Three Fingers' hand moved up inside his jacket.

Joran said, 'You should do something about that itch on your shoulder, mate.'

After he had left, Tick Tock said, 'Smart arse bastard! I'm going to blow his nuts off before we leave.'

They decided the graveyard was a dead end, so that night they would check out the church.

Chapter Ten

Even without snow, February is England's coldest season with freezing temperatures, rain and icy winds. Tonight would be a reconnaissance to find a warm, suitable, secret place far enough away from getting sent home, for Rosie and Hanna to have a fag at midnight. They snuck out through the skylight on the bedroom roof with their torches and went through the church to the graveyard where the faint sound of the wind whistled among the headstones.

The rain and darkness covered the tombstones in an eerie mist, the only light coming from their torches. They took refuge in an overhead opening where steps went down to one of the graveyard crypts. Shivering, they hunched their shoulders, crossed their arms and snuggled into each other against the cold. The door was old and bent and had a carved inscription: '1642, their souls will remain in England forever.'

'We could squeeze through the door,' Rosie said, 'and get out of the cold, and check the place out for the future. They'll never find us down here having a fag, and it's warm.'

They squeezed through the door and shone their torches around. There were unlit kerosene lamps along the wall. They were in a large square room with four metal coffins sitting on marble structures, inscribed as follows.

The Honourable Menzi Munda, first chancellor Manor
Mansion, RIP 1602
Lady Munda, RIP 1602
Master Huene Munda, 14 years RIP 1602
Drowned in the sinking of a sailing vessel in the Thames

The passage seemed to carry on for quite a way. Along the passageway were individual shelves dug into the walls with metal caskets and candles in a jar that had long ago burnt down. As they walked along in the light of the torch, Rosie placed a cigarette on every second casket shelf.

'Why are you doing that?' asked Hanna.

'To make sure we don't get lost down here. We won't get caught with them in our room, and we can smoke them one by one each time we come back. They'll never find us down here having a fag.'

In another crypt off the passage were eight caskets with four, round, two-inch holes in the top of them.

'Why have they got holes?' asked Rosie.

'They're called viewing caskets,' said Hanna. 'The holes let the fresh air in to the bodies, so they don't smell when you open them for the viewing, then the body is taken out if it's going to be burnt or placed in a coffin for burial.'

They began opening the caskets. The first one was empty as expected, but when they opened the second one, they jumped back.

'Jesus Christ!' they said.

There was a man in there. The inscription on his shirt read "Liam Finnigan, graveyard maintenance". There was a nun in the third casket dressed in her religious habit, scapular, cincture, coif and veil.

A voice said, 'That's Sister Margarita sleeping peacefully. She was replaced by me on instructions from The Syndicate. I'm not a real nun, but I'm good at it, don't you think, girls? You will soon be caught. Shut up and get in the caskets.'

She closed and fastened the lids on them and left.

*

Three Fingers and his cronies were in the church, having just discovered a concealed trapdoor with brass pull rings on the floor where the pulpit and the priest stood. They swung the door up on its hinges and went down into the crypt.

'Someone has been down here recently,' said Dolly. 'There's a candle still burning at that casket in the wall.'

They went over to get the candle and saw the inscription. Dolly read it out loud: "Money and jewellery are the sins of God. RIP forever, 2008." This one's only two years old,' she said.

'Yeah, big deal,' said Tick Tock. 'Grab the candle and let's keep looking.'

As they got further down the crypt passageway, they could hear muffled voices. They crept along close to the wall with their guns drawn. When they got to the large crypt room, they could hear the voices were coming from two caskets. They opened them and two girls jumped out.

'Christ, who are you?' Three Fingers said.

They told them they were from the girl's college at the convent and were down here having a fag when a nun came and shoved them in the caskets.

'Sounds like bullshit to me,' said Dolly, 'You're up to no

good down here. The nun knew what you were looking for, which is obviously what she was also looking for, and more likely knows where it is and what it is. I think we'll just keep you in those caskets till we find out what's going on, and who's responsible for what around here.'

They were pushed back into the caskets and Three Fingers and his mob went back through the church and left.

Chapter Eleven

Back in Australia, the Spiders, especially Joe, had been following the action as it unfolded. Harrigan passed it on to each of them, who were now all back in their own homes.

Joe rang Max and said, 'Did you get the latest on Hambleden?'

'Yes,' Max said. 'Looks like things are hotting up, and three more players have arrived for the party. The big worry is those two girls who have gone missing.'

'I think we should go there.'

'Joe, you're the bloke who thinks he's the knight in shining armour. Only trouble is, mate, knights don't exist anymore.'

'Well, I've always said the two most important days of your life are the day you were born and the day you find out why. People like you and me were for just these occasions, like the last mission we did. It's all about helping those who are less fortunate than us.'

'Bugger you, Joe, you always manage to get me with sensible and slippery arguments. Okay, ring around and see if you can get everyone back this weekend. I'm not having anything to do with it. You will have to do all the tap dancing to convince everyone, particularly the girls. Remember – one in, all in. One goes, we all go. You might have to use that line.'

'Don't know how he did it,' Max said to Jane later, 'but they'll all be here this weekend. What do you think about all this?'

Jane said, 'There is a lot to consider. For example, we are far too old now for getting into anything robust that required a lot of energy, or dangerous situations with shooting and fighting. You blokes need to convince yourselves that part of your life is well past. As good as you all used to be, it's over. And you shouldn't be doing anything your guardian angel can't do. If you want my answer, it's this: if we are going for a two-week holiday with some treasure hunting and history research in a quiet English country town, then I'm all for it. But if there's any chance it's anything else, I would be against anyone going.'

By Saturday lunchtime, they had all arrived and were sitting in the Lobster Cave restaurant quietly consuming a lobster cooked to their own liking. Max had lobster thermidor, Jane had hers grilled, Bruce and Joe had theirs mornay, and Sue and Lois had theirs grilled and mixed with macaroni and cheese.

The time had come to discuss what they were all there for, so they did it with a $120 bottle of Penfolds Reserve Bin A Chardonnay. Joe had convinced them to go to Hambleden, but the deal was this. They were definitely going only for a holiday for a bit of treasure hunting and research, and to enjoy the countryside of a small English village wrapped in history and stories of long-ago pirates, cut-throats and shady characters. The girls were looking forward to the centuries-old church and houses. But if anything happened while they were there, the boys were made to promise they would leave it to the police and the proper authorities.

Bruce and Joe nodded their head and said, 'No worries, we will,' but Max didn't believe it, not for one minute. He knew their minds were already in top gear.

43

Chapter Twelve

When they got off their Qantas flight in London at 6.30 am, the temperature was somewhat different from their last stop in Singapore.

Sue and Lois said, 'We've only been here five minutes and we're bloody freezing!'

'Well, get used to it, girls,' said Max. 'We are here for two weeks.'

The keys to the hire car and cottage were at the Hertz desk, and soon they were on their way. It was an easy drive, with plenty of room for the six of them in the Land Rover Discovery. The girls kept whinging till the heater was turned up full bore.

The Spiders arrived in the small, dreamy village of Hambleden about 11 am. They decided to find the cottage in Cherry Blossom Lane and put their things away before going to lunch somewhere.

As they drove along, they opened the car windows. It was bitterly cold, and it made their skin glow. Nature had opened her cold lungs and gave them that tingling sensation and pain in their fingers, even though they had gloves on, and when they exhaled the warm air from their lungs, they looked like they were all smoking.

Max said, 'Anything with two or four legs will be somewhere warm.'

The countryside was fresh and green, but nature was already reminding them they would never be part of it. They were just passing through history, permitted to look and admire. It reminded them all how nature could tend to all things big and small, like the blankets of snow on rooftops and trees, nature quietly caressing the branches till they lost some of their extra weight with the snow falling gently to earth. And then Max saw it – the countyside was not all green. At the base of the distant mountains and on the skyline were a variety of many colours. If you moved your head up to the horizon and back down to the meadow, the view changed, like looking into a cardboard kaleidoscope.

The old-fashioned cottage looked wonderful, with its dressed flint and red brick, thatched roof and broken picket fence, all holding silent memories and secrets of years gone by. The old timber frames holding up the porch, and cane chairs invited them in. The cottage was in perfect harmony with the surrounding lush countryside and distant mountains, wild Scotch thistles, heather (known also as ling) and a variety of flowers that grew all round. All it lacked was a stream full of trout.

There was no dishwasher nor separate showers, but the minute they walked in the door, they knew it was perfect. The atmosphere was just so relaxing and calming. The cottage had been furnished respecting its age with a mixture of original old and second-hand furniture from London. It reminded Jane of the gingerbread house she had made when she was a child.

She said, 'We will have a peaceful and restful stay in this

dreamy little cottage that has come straight from a child's storybook.'

The Stag and Huntsman pub looked like the place for lunch. Six people walking into a small local pub in any town is bound to attract attention, particularly now with the mystery three and the man calling himself Joran, and now two girls missing from the Catholic college at the old convent. This meant, in the last couple of weeks, there were now ten new faces in the village.

'And that's very unusual,' said the bartender to Paddy and Stewart, who were having a pint of Guinness at the bar. 'These people are popping up like mushrooms after rain.'

'We haven't got any of them pegged yet,' said Paddy, 'but I'll bet, London to a brick, they are retired tourists in their very late seventies, probably staying at the MacAlister cottage.'

Paddy and Stewart couldn't help themselves. Curiosity may have killed the cat, but they went over to meet them anyway.

'Hello! I'm Stewart MacGregor and this here is young Paddy O'Flarity.' (Young Paddy was probably in his late sixties.) 'Are you holidaymakers?

Lois answered as usual and said, 'Yes, we are from Melbourne in Australia. We have been reading about the history of this little village and its rumours of pirates and treasures and its century-old buildings and old houses. We are staying in one in Cherry Blossom Lane.'

'Yes,' Stewart said, 'that's the old MacAlister cottage. Nice old place, often gets rented out. How long will you be staying with us?'

'Two weeks,' Sue said, 'unless we find all the treasure and buy the village.'

They all laughed. Suddenly a loud whistle blew.

Jane said, 'That's loud. What's that for?'

Paddy said, 'That, my dear, is the noonday whistle, used here in years gone by to tell the workers and the schoolchildren it was time to stop for lunch. It has been kept up by the town for old time's sake, to keep some of the past alive. Everyone sets their watch by it and stops for lunch.'

'Well, if we can be of any help, just come and see us,' said Stewart. 'Paddy is the graveyard caretaker, and I am the caretaker at the lady's college in the old convent.'

'Have they found those two young girls yet?' said Jane.

'No, they haven't,' said Paddy.

They went back to the bar and told the bartender, 'They'll no find any treasure, but they will have fun looking at all the old buildings and reading journals to find where the treasure might be. We've nothing to fear from those nice old people.'

Chapter Thirteen

Sergeant Weir and an inspector from London were interviewing young Clara and Edith, with Sister Theresa present.

The girls knew Rosie and Hanna had gone out for a smoke the night they had disappeared, but they did not want to get them sent home for smoking. So they said, 'Sometimes they would go for a walk at night and take us with them just for the fresh air. But we were too tired to go that night. We would only go out to the seat on the lawn. And when we woke up the next morning, they weren't here,' and they started crying.

Sister Theresa said, 'Don't upset yourselves, ladies. We will no doubt find them soon. They may have even gone to London for some fun and are having trouble getting back. We have spoken to their parents, and the girls did not say they were returning home. But we will find them, I am sure.'

*

Three Fingers and The Syndicate mob were in the town hall looking through old newspapers and clippings when the Spiders walked in and asked at the desk for any journals or clippings relating to the histories of the graveyard, church and flour mill. They were sent in the direction of the three goons, who were sitting near the storage shelves.

Three Fingers said, 'Well, the treasure is here somewhere all right. There are six more looking for it——'

'—and six more to do away with,' said Tick Tock.

Sue walked back to the desk and spoke again to the town clerk.

'There's not much written about the flour mill, is there?'

'In one of the journals, there is a mention of it by that pirate, Calico Jack, on the day he was hanged,' Dee, the town clerk, said, 'but I'll tell you what I know if you like.'

She made them cups of tea and they sat down to listen.

'The mill was recorded in the Doomsday book of 1086, which was written to record England's land and wealth. The mill was owned by Queen Matilda in those days and had a rent of 20 shillings per year. The mill yielded 1000 eels per year. The oldest part of the building was built in the late eighteenth century, incorporating parts of the seventeenth-century mill. In the late nineteenth century, a barge called *Maid of the Mill* took flour to a biscuit factory each week and returned with broken biscuits to sell to the villagers. The mill was still operating in the 1950s; however, it fell out of use in the 1970s and was converted into apartments. The waterwheel was converted to turbine which still turns the paddlewheel, more for show now than anything else. But it's good for the kids that still fish there not far from the base of the wheel where the water is churned up, providing the small fish with fresh oxygen as they swim by or hang around.'

They went back and found the journal with Calico Jack's last words and read it a couple of times.

What do you think?' said Lois.

'The ravings of a man about to die,' said Bruce, 'nothing in it.'

They had also learnt that Calico Jack and Mary Read were buried in Port Royal, so there would be no grave here, but there could easily be a grave somewhere here for Anne Bonny.

It was still bitterly cold, so they decided to retreat to their seventeenth-century cottage for the afternoon until the evening meal, where they had booked a table for six at the Manor House. When they were all warm and comfortable, enjoying a sweet sherry, there was a knock on the door.

'I'll get it,' said Jane.

There was a delightful and fascinating eighty-something woman with wisps of white hair at the door. She had a gentle and kind demeanour. *These lovely attributes only come with age*, Jane thought. Her skin was wrinkled, which showed she had spent more time on earth than most, but she wore her years of experience with pride. You could tell she was a lovely lady inside a worn-out body.

Jane was gone for some time at the door. When she returned, she said, 'I think you will want to hear what this lady's got to say.'

They offered her a sherry which she accepted. She took a deep breath, and said, 'My name is Anne Campbell, I am eighty-two years old and I'm a direct descendent of Anne Bonny.'

'What!' they cried. 'Does anyone else know that?'

'No.'

'So why are you telling us? We're not from here.'

'Do you know a man called Harrigan?'

'Yes.'

'That's exactly why I'm telling you,' and she went on. 'My mother's great-great-grandmother was Anne Bonny's baby girl. I have listened to many stories over the years that have come down through my family about where the treasure is hidden. None of them were right, of course. The information and locations have changed many times over the years. However, I believe I know exactly where most of it is. Our secret family information was that Anne came back here and moved some of the silver pennies to support her lifestyle travel. But my mother told me she came back here to die and was buried by her two grandchildren in a secret underground place known only to the family.'

'Do you know that location?' asked Max.

'Yes, I do, but first, there are certain actions and papers to sign if I am to go ahead and trust you people from Australia and take you to my great-great-great grandmother's grave. I am not without connections with certain Australian authorities. You have told me you are familiar with a man called Harrigan?'

'Yes, we are,' they said.

'Well, he is also a distant relative of Calico Jack and Anne Bonny. His parents moved to Australia when he was fourteen years old. He has told me you are most trustworthy. I have been to London and had documents drawn up for you to sign in regard to non-disclosure of what you have and will be told. However, there is a release clause. If war comes, the treasure is to be recovered and used to support homeless children, or for any other reason it is deemed essential by your group, the Spiders. It is to be handled by the church and yourselves –not the greedy government!'

*

They were sitting at their dinner table at the Manor House when Tick Tock, Three Fingers and Dolly came into the dining room and sat down only one table away.

'Jesus,' Max whispered, 'look at these goons, hatched out of a prehistoric egg somewhere on a blanket in the sun. Why aren't they put out of their misery at birth? They just reek of the smell of death and murder. Look at the moll – she's almost got some clothes on, and she's got those jail tattoos on her arms. They are cannon fodder for whoever they work for. Anyone want to have a guess who?'

'The Syndicate,' they said simultaneously.

Max continued. 'The one in the pinstripe suit sees himself as some sort of Al Capone. The larger one with the slimy grin is a prime example of an expendable item and probably spent three years in the fourth grade. Whoever they are, they are trouble, and we need to keep away from them.'

The deal with the girls had been no guns, but Bruce and Joe had decided going so far away, it wasn't up for discussion, so they had packed theirs and told nobody.

Chapter Fourteen

There was a sombre feeling within the college since Rosie and Hanna had disappeared. Three out of the four nuns feared something bad had happened, and the Mother Superior was beside herself. Nothing like this had ever happened before. The girls lost interest in everything. Tonight, they were going to London for a final dinner critique, but the news of the missing girls would affect their performance at the dinner. Stewart drove the bus to the front entrance, the girls and three nuns climbed in and they set off for London.

Down in the crypt, Hanna and Rosie were long past crying, but at least they could talk to each other. Their voices carried through the holes in the caskets.

'Are we going to die here, Hanna?'

'No, Rosie. Someone will come.'

*

Joran had done the research he had come there for. He entered the crypt through the church trapdoor that he had watched the goons go through three nights ago. He had heard everything they had said, so he knew exactly where he was going. He went down the wooden steps, turned on his torch and there it was, over in its cradle in the wall, just like he had heard them say. He went over and read the short inscription and date: two years ago, 2008, sounded about right. He heard a noise and turned around.

'So that's who you are,' she said, 'I had The Syndicate check you out, "AAA Diamond Insurance Investigator" Joran Clark. But in fact, you are ASIS, Australian Secret Intelligence Service. Take a good look around. You're going to be spending a lot of time down here, but unfortunately you'll be dead. The diamond mine owned by Rosie's family has been shipping diamonds from Africa to Hambleden for delivery to a client in Marlow. None of the shipments have successfully been received by the client, but have been traced as far as Hambleden, eleven shipments in total. You will be dead shortly, so it's only fair that you see what you came for.'

She opened the casket and there they were, sparkling and glistening in the torchlight. But they were only the diamonds she had been given; there were a lot more elsewhere. There was also silver pennies and bundles of pound notes.

She said, 'The silver pennies and money are part of Calico Jack's treasure. When Anne Bonny came back, she split most of the treasure into several locations. The old curate in the church at the time saw where Anne had hidden that parcel of the treasure. He wrote the location down and before he died, passed the sealed envelope to his priest for safekeeping. The envelope was passed along from priest to priest over the years with none of them aware of the contents.'

She said she'd stumbled on the envelope among old bibles and prayer books four years ago when she had been sent here by The Syndicate. She had eliminated Sister Margarita, who was sick anyway. The nuns thought she had gone to London, and although not a nun, she had taken Margarita's place.

'So, why are you hoarding all this?' Joran said.

'The world is changing – I can feel it everywhere – and we need the strength and the will to rid the earth of the impurities of wealth, money and diamonds that promote theft, prostitution and division in the classes. They promote the domination of one person controlling all others, and that's when the age of the dictators will be born, and one by one, people will fall to the power and domination that money and diamonds brings. There will come a time in this world called the "diamond devastation".'

Then she shot him.

He was dragged along the crypt passage to where the viewing caskets were.

'Hello, girls. I have brought you some company. No good talking to him. He's not a very good talker, probably because he's dead.'

She put him in one of the empty caskets and left.

*

The Spiders drove the ninety minutes back to London with eighty-two-year-old Anne to the lawyer's office to sign the non-disclosure agreements. Anne said she would meet them all tomorrow, and as promised, tell and show them what she knew to be true.

'You see,' she said, 'historians often stray from the truth.'

*

The dinner in London, although sombre and quiet, was seen as a success. The college girls were now sitting quietly in the bus waiting for Stewart to drive them back. There was a large trailer attached to the bus with a big wooden crate and some sort of cargo covered with canvas. Four Asian men and three females jumped on the bus just as Stewart arrived.

'Who the hell are you?' he said.

'Shut up,' they said, shot him in the head and drove off with the girls.

The London port stretches along the banks of the Thames between London and the North Sea. Once it was the largest port in the world, and that's where the sailing vessel, the *Mary Jane*, an old merchant cargo ship, was waiting with its large loading ramp open to the dock. There were visible signs of the old ship's working days of trudging up and down the North Sea.

The bus with the girls drove straight up the ramp and on to the ship. The ramp was pulled up and became part of the ship again. With one long blast and three short ones, she went astern of the dock and was gone, gliding silently and effortlessly into the North Sea, giving the impression this was what she had been dreaming of for days. She was old but as solid as the big oak she was made from. Her sails were as white as snow, and with the favourable winds, they plunged her bow deep into the trough of the waves with pride, to reappear through the top of the wave with her bow in the air and a massive spray of water that covered the foredeck. The huge oak mast that once held branches and leaves now held the weight of the full-blown sails, as the skipper on the rudder chose a path of his own through the ever changing currents of the sea.

Now they were far enough out, Stewart MacGregor's body was thrown overboard. They had long ago lost the sight of land, and the ocean stretched out in front of them in a seemingly endless expanse of blues, greens and rainbow colours produced by the sun on the water that merged with the distant skyline, surface ripples going every which way in the current and chilly breeze. Fresh clean air and the smell and taste of sea salt was present everywhere – if you weren't one of the twenty-two girls in the hull, locked in cages for their journey to who knew where. Apart from the girls, who were eventually going to several places, the ship's cargo was only one crate, the stolen gold, and fifteen barrels of rum for the black market. The entire journey would take several weeks.

*

The three nuns who had not been taken were being interviewed at Scotland Yard by detectives and the Secret Intelligence Services (SIS), also known as MI6. The nuns knew nothing and were driven back to Hambleden to the college to find the Mother Superior in her bed with her brass crucifix inserted into her neck. Her eyes were staring at the ceiling, her thin bony hands stiff and cold, clutching the crucifix in a seemingly last effort to survive.

She had been dead for several days.

Chapter Fifteen

/\/hy is it we seem to have the knack to keep walking into someone else's shit storm? Here we are on a simple treasure hunt holiday, and now we are smack bang in the middle of it all. Christ, who would steal twenty-two young women? One woman is hard enough to handle,' said Joe.

'Be very careful, smart arse,' said Lois, 'And why did I ever think the Spiders could go anywhere without being involved in some sort of shit fight?'

They met with Anne as promised. They sat on the church seat near the gates to the graveyard.

She said, 'My mother was told by her mother that Anne Bonny escaped the hangman because she was pregnant. She befriended a jailer, known only as Ryan, with the promise of a share in the treasure if he helped her escape. The two of them slipped away one night and sailed back here to Hambleden on a sailing vessel called *The Black Hawk* where they settled in among the village folk. Neither of them had been seen here before. It is said that she was seen at the church praying. That's not true. Nobody knew who she was; they had never seen her – another example of historians playing with the truth. So, they were not known by the troopers and could move around freely. Some of the illegal stolen coins in the treasure were secretly exchanged in London for legal tender they could safely use here in Hambleden.

'I am the only one left in the family who has this information, passed down over many years by family members, and more likely to be correct than what has been written by someone who thinks they know the history of Anne Bonny. I watched them build this seat here that we are sitting on. It was very concerning, because under this seat, as you will see from a letter written by Bonny to her daughter, my great-great-grandmother, are 200 silver coins and one double leopard coin worth four million pounds in today's world. Let's walk and talk for a while on our way to a very special cottage.'

They were walking down Cherry Blossom Lane. The Spiders all looked at each other.

'Can't be, can it?' said Auntie.

While they all stood outside the cottage they had rented, Anne said, 'This cottage is known now as the MacAlister Cottage, but go back far enough and you will find it was built and owned by a Mr and Mrs Ryan Campbell, otherwise known as Bonny and Ryan. Nobody knew that then, nor do they know that now. There is a dry well at the back of the house that has long ago been covered over and now houses a thick vegetable garden. In some of Bonny's letters later in life, she writes that she is very much enjoying looking after her very expensive vegetable garden. Take from that what you may. Mind you, Calico Jack had another stash that he moved somewhere here just before he was caught. Who knows where that would be? And then there's the golden eagle. Who knows where that would be, if it's here at all?'

The Spiders were dumbfounded with what they had just heard.

'I am going to take you now to my special place in the world, Anne Bonny's grave. Can we go in your car?'

'Of course we can,' they said.

They were in the middle of nowhere, kilometres from the village, and standing under a magnificent clump of large birch trees. A flock of black birds flew overhead. Jane closed her eyes and tried to put herself in this exact spot 200 years ago. The sunken grave under the trees was surrounded by a high, old, rusty wrought iron fence with what long ago had sharp points. There was a large old stump, easily a metre in diameter, with the signs of age visible by the amount of rotting that had occurred There was no grass growing around the stump, which seemed unusual as the grass was plentiful everywhere else, kept down over the years by sheep grazing nearby. The new and old yellow fallen birch leaves lay upon the grass, and like the woman in the grave, some had withered and were decaying.

The gravestone looked so cold, lonely and worn. Anne showed them a small, hardly readable inscription on the back of the headstone that simply said, "Bonny". The words were almost gone from centuries of harsh weather lashing the grave. But after some scrutinising, they were able to read the words:

I hope you find a better life than the one you have left.
Death is only a shadow, and I will join you soon, my love.
Ryan.
RIP Anne Campbell, 1784, gone to God.
Their research in London told them, among other things ,

that Ryan Campbell had died in 1794, ten years after Bonny. So, where was he buried? Presumably not here with her.

Chapter Sixteen

Back to the college came Scotland Yard, MI6 and a team from the ASIS with a high-powered man from Australia called Lieutenant Commander Harrigan, whom the Spiders had worked with in the past and knew most of them personally.

Harrigan said to the ASIS team, 'I have engaged the conference room at the Stag and Huntsman tonight for a plan of action, and have invited the well-known, old, but brilliant crime solving Spiders who just happen to be here on a two-week holiday.'

They all said, 'Good. We will look forward to seeing them again, particularly those two dags, Bruce and Joe.'

The Spiders told them what they knew, minus what they had signed to keep secret in the Bonny affair. They all agreed they couldn't see the treasure and murders here at Hambleden having anything to do with the recent disappearance of the girls in the bus.

'Jesus,' Harrigan said, 'how does someone pinch twenty-two girls in London under everyone's nose and no one sees anything? Begs belief! Tonight, we will set the priorities and select groups to undertake those areas. Have dinner and I will see you all at 8 pm at the pub.'

Harrigan spoke to the Spiders outside the pub and said he knew they were just here on a holiday, but he was happy for them to be involved in the investigation as much or as little as they wished. The meeting was held and groups given their role. The Spiders said they were happy to just poke around till something jumped out, as it usually did. They had been talking about Calico Jack's last words in the journal for several days now; they decided to go back and copy his words exactly from the journal and take it and themselves to the waterwheel mill , as they might be able to uncover a secret clue in his pointed comments about the mill.

*

Unknown to the Spiders and Anne, the three goons had followed them to the secluded grave under the birch trees and were content to watch from a distance. When the Spiders and Anne had left the grave, the goons went to look.

'What a waste of time this trip has been,' said Tick Tock, 'Who the hell is Anne Campbell? She's got bugger all to do with what we're looking for; just some farm woman's old grave from the past.'

The goons drove back to town where, coming out of the general store, was Anne.

'There she is now,' said Dolly.

'Right. Grab her,' said Three Fingers, 'get her in the car.'

They asked her what all the interest in the grave under the tree was all about. She said it was her great-great-grandmother's grave which she often tended.

'Bullshit!' said Dolly, 'So, why were those others there?'

'They are counting and logging graves in the area, and I wanted my great-great-grandmother's grave logged as well. Being out here by itself, I was worried it would not be counted and logged along with the others that they will count and log tonight at the graveyard in private with no one around to annoy them.'

They took her back to the grave and tied her to the old wrought iron fence around the grave and said, 'We are going to pay the graveyard a visit tonight, and we will see what those geriatrics have to say. They won't be hard to deal with. Try not to freeze to death before we come back tomorrow.'

*

The Spiders found themselves at the gates of the graveyard. It was a dark and scary night.

Max said, 'It's not the scariest place I've ever been, but it would go close. Everyone knows that graveyard headstones at night are a breeding ground for ghosts of the departed to find closure.'

The rain fell softly on the newly dug soil of a grave, patting it down like the soft bare feet of a small child. The flowers were fresh, unlike many others with their dried flowers tucked into a glass jar. And here and there the old tombstones were leaning towards each other like the family and friends buried below. What they were doing here in the dark and the rain was not ideal but necessary for what they needed to do without prying eyes. They were looking for other graves with the name Campbell on them to enable them to link up history with any other deceased relatives of eighty-two-year-old Anne Campbell. Lois and

Jane said they believed there was a lot more to this story than Anne had revealed.

There was an Audrey and Alfred Campbell, buried together. He and his wife had died the same day in 1846. Their ages were not carved on the headstone; however, the records in London had shown she was sixty-two and he was seventy-one. Both had been stabbed to death, and the killer never found. A weather-beaten headstone next to theirs read, "Henry and Edith Campbell, their kindness will be remembered forever", and the words, "Ryan has gone to join Anne".

Jane said, 'Whatever happened here more than two hundred years ago is silent history and can never be changed. The truth may never surface, and most of what people are told or written by historians is bullshit written as a fill-in for the real truth of history they can't find.'

They were somewhat separated looking for graves when the three goons arrived.

They came up behind Max and Jane with their guns drawn and said, 'Fancy's meeting you here. Start talking about what you're doing.'

Max said, 'My old uncle, Mick O'Reilly, in 1720 buried his canary and money with him in his grave. We are waiting and listening for the canary to whistle and tell us which grave is his.'

'We will help you listen,' said Tick Tock.

'Shut up, you idiot!' said Three Fingers.

Joe and Bruce came up behind the goons with their guns drawn, the guns that Bruce and Joe weren't supposed to have.

Bruce said, 'If I were you, lady, and you, propeller neck with the bow tie, and you too, bone head, I would drop the guns and get as far away from here as you can.'

'Who are you?' the goons said.

Lois said, 'We are the Spiders of Spy, here simply on a holiday, and we don't need to see you fools again.'

After the goons were released from the graveyard by the Spiders, Lois said to Joe and Bruce, 'We agreed no guns and gung-ho stuff. I'm an idiot for believing you two could follow rules.'

*

The next day, they had two places to go: London, to find the grave's registration to follow the family burial tree, and whatever they could get about the unsolved murders of the husband and wife together in the grave; then back to the waterwheel mill to decipher Calico's death scribbles, written on the day of his hanging so long ago. Being at the same place that he was describing when he wrote his last words might help to decipher the scribbles he had left as a possible clue, if that's what his words were about. Or else they were just the memories and ravings of a man about to die, and nothing else.

Chapter Seventeen

A shipment of gold bars had been stolen from the Bank of London almost a year ago by high-ranking members of The Syndicate and hidden away, waiting the opportunity to be transported overseas to a destination known only on the dark web. Packed in a wooden crate and worth eight million English pounds, it weighed several tonnes.

When The Syndicate learnt of the girl's college dinner from the nun who was their undercover operative at the college, they put their plan into action. The crate was on a hydraulic trolley and placed in the storeroom at the restaurant, along with the restaurant owner who had got cold feet and had had her throat cut. While the girls were at their dinner, the gold had been loaded behind the bus on a heavy-duty trailer. Now the gold bars with twenty-two girls and the bus were on their way overseas, nestled in the hull of the *Mary Jane*. They could have done the same thing with the empty bus while the girls were at dinner, but the girls were security against any harsh action by the authorities until they reached their destination for the gold. The girls were a separate issue. Girls of high income families were worth a lot of money on the human trade market, and that money would be shared among the crew of the *Mary Jane*.

Down in the hull of the ship, which was putrid and had a vile smell of vomit mixed with the smell of the kegs of rum on their way to the black market, the girls in the cages had all been violently sick.

The greasy little Asian with one ear said, 'Filthy women' as he hosed them all along with the cages. 'Don't worry, girlies,' he said as he threw in twenty-two cans of bully beef that had been opened. 'You're on your way to a new life.'

*

The Spiders had returned from London, and while they hadn't got all the burial information they expected, the trip had not been wasted.

It was a lovely sunny day, but the cold wind was spoiling it. They were sitting on the bank of the large wooden waterwheel channel and watching the wooden paddles pushing the water along the channel for its old friend, the mill. They weren't to know that the goons had not disappeared but were hiding and watching from behind the waterwheel. The leaves from several birch trees were being pushed around by the breeze, orange, green and yellow silently falling, adding to the charm of this old mill. The little grebes, or dabchicks, were zipping through and around the spray of the water as it came from the paddles.

Lois said, 'I feel like I'm watching my life continuously moving in circles but going nowhere.'

There were the usual band of small kids fishing in the waterwheel channel. They were fishing not far from the base of the wheel where the paddles churned up the water, providing fresh oxygen for the small fish as they swam by or hung around. The Spiders heard a scream and saw that a little boy had fallen into the water channel and was being pushed along the short distance in the current towards the wheel. Max rushed over to dive into the channel, but to his surprise, Tick Tock had seen what had happened, and he was already in the channel, holding the boy up. The two of them were almost at the wheel, being pushed along in the water by the paddles on the wheel. He managed to throw the little boy out of the channel just as he was sucked under the wheel. When the wheel came round each time, Tick Tock's head was pushed in and out between two large wooden paddles. He looked like a demented cuckoo, with his neck obviously broken. When the wheel came round for the fourth time, two paddles either side of his head had split apart and silver coins were spewing into the channel.

Jane was yelling out, 'Shut the wheel down! Hurry up, shut the wheel down!'

As far as Tick Tock was concerned, he had probably done the most honourable thing in his rotten life. Three Fingers and Dolly had long gone.

Max said, 'See, it's an ill wind that blows no good. We have found some of the treasure that Calico split up, and Tick Tock has done us a favour by removing himself from the planet Earth, a task we would have had to do eventually.'

The police arrived along with Lieutenant Commander Harrigan.

Sergeant Johno Weir said to the Spiders, 'I knew you lot were trouble. I just didn't know when it was going to happen. We will turn the wheel off and send a diver in to collect the coins from the water channel and the wheel. This might put an end to all the rumours – although there doesn't seem enough for it to be called treasure; just plain and simple theft, if you ask me.'

'Well, we have reliable information that tell us that this small lot came from the main lot, but why it was hidden here, we may never know. But find it and put the split lots together,' said Max, 'and it's more than just theft. And even if the rest isn't found, some of these coins are worth a fortune. There will be quite a few million pounds in this small lot.'

*

Three Fingers and Dolly were on their way back to Bonny's grave to give Anne the third degree, if she hadn't died from the cold overnight. The last hundred metres had to be done on foot, once through the fence into the meadow. They pushed their way through long grass where dragonflies hovered over wildflowers like miniature helicopters. The sun was warm on their backs and a light breeze ruffled their hair; it was one of those warm days not often felt and seen at this time of year.

Anne had been released from the grave fence by a local farmer out rabbiting, who had just seen the goons coming carrying guns. Anne was hiding behind a blackberry bush, too scared to move and jumping at the slightest sound. One foot in front of the other, the goons kicked up small insects and critters hiding in the long grass. There was a loud rifle shot, and a small red hole appeared in the middle of Three Finger's forehead and a larger one at the back where a 7.62 round came spiralling out. He stood there staring for a moment, then fell face down among the dead leaves and insects. Dolly went to ground and started crawling back in the long grass to the vehicle. Whoever had fired had a long-range rifle, so the .38 snub nose that she kept in her bra would be useless.

She needed to go into hiding and notify The Syndicate for extra help. Whether they would come or not was another thing. Once she got back to the village, her cover would be blown. She thought the church would be the best place to go while she gathered her thoughts. She had only been there for fifteen minutes when a nun came into the church and sat beside her.

She said, 'Are you well, my child?'

'No,' she said. 'I have lost many treasures in life, and another two of them today, Sister.'

'Do not worry, my child. You will be staying at the college with me until we find your treasure.'

Chapter Eighteen

'What is it with these Poms?' Joe said. 'They live in a freezing climate, so they're used to the cold, but they drink warm beer that's supposed to be drunk cold.'

It was late afternoon and the Spiders were in the Stag and Huntsman. The girls were drinking coffee and the boys were having a scotch when the door of the pub opened, and along with the breeze, Anne Campbell came in.

'Jesus,' Jane said, 'she looks terrible!'

She came over and sat down.

'What's happened?' Lois said, 'You look bloody awful. What are those red chafe marks on your wrists?'

'I was tied up all night at the grave by those thugs that came to town. The woman and the one with the missing fingers came back this morning and the farmer that untied me shot the man dead. The woman crawled off in the long grass. I have contacted Sergeant Weir; he is on his way here now.'

The door opened again to signal the arrival of the "cavalry". The sergeant and two bobbies sat down, and they heard the story all over again.

*

Even though the nun and Dolly were both agents from The Syndicate, neither of them knew; agents were never told if they had other agents in the same area unless they had been sent together.

'Come into the vestibule, dear, and we will talk,' the nun said.

They sat down and the nun said, 'So, tell me about this treasure you have lost, my dear. It's important that we find what you have lost.'

'What has been lost is of no importance. It's what has not been found that's desperately important. If I fail to find it, the people who hired me will kill me very quickly, I can assure you,' Dolly said.

The nun said, as she put her hand under her habit, 'Yes, I'm afraid they will, my child.'

She shot Dolly through the left eyeball.

I've got to try and get rid of that pull to the left when I fire, she said to herself.

*

The priest came in later that night to prepare his sermon and fell over the body in the dark.

'Mary, mother of Jesus!' and because he thought there was no one else there, he also said. 'Fuck, who's this?'

He would study his notes on the pulpit, and then he would report the murder. The nun had hidden in the vestibule when she heard the priest coming. The priest was packing up his books when a poisoned feather dart buried itself into the back of his head. He fell over the top of the pulpit, looked up at the nun and said, 'You!' and he was dead.

The nun dragged the two bodies through the trapdoor in the floor down to the crypt chambers and left through the graveyard crypt entrance.

*

Why are all these people being murdered in this sleepy forgotten village?' said Johno, 'Let's get those bloody Spiders on to this, if they're so good. I do not care if they are just on holidays. The government agents are busy with the missing girl's case, and their investigations have all come to dead ends.'

Harrigan met with the spiders.

They said, 'If someone pays our rent, we'll come on board.'

'Consider it done,' Harrigan said, 'So ... why are you still sitting here?'

'Yes, sir,' they said, 'Hardly a challenge!'

Harrigan knew there was now going to be big time action in town.

Bruce said, 'There are plenty of places in a place like this to start looking for answers that the police over the years have sat on their arse and couldn't be bothered finding, and those that were interested were shut down by corrupt police in high places tied to The Syndicate.'

'The first place I would look,' said Auntie, 'would be that church and Catholic girls college. That's just the place no one would want to interfere with, so it's just the place we should.'

It was Sunday and the church bells were ringing, telling the village that the service would commence in thirty minutes. Three nuns filed in and took up their place front left of the church. The fourth nun had said she was unwell and was absent. The organ stopped playing, but the priest was nowhere to be seen. The next day, the police searched the small house he lived in at the back of the church and found nothing that would explain his absence from the service the day before.

*

The Spiders sat together at the pub with Johno and Harrigan.

Max said, 'I think this might be the plan of attack. What sort of weapons do you have at the station?'

'Everyone in our group is licensed for most assault weapons,' Johno said. 'One 7.62 assault rifle, one four-shot shotgun and four .38 revolvers, so what do you need?'

'Jane is the best shot with the rifle. Bruce is the worst shot with everything, so he gets the shotgun. The rest of us are crack shots with handguns. The quicker we get the weapons from you the quicker we begin sorting this jigsaw puzzle out. There won't be too many to kill as most or all of them are already dead. I suspect there's two of them: the one that's still doing the killing and a Syndicate agent.'

Johno said, 'Come and sign for them tomorrow, and Lieutenant Commander Harrigan can sign the request.'

Max said, 'I'm thinking Bruce with the shotgun goes with Auntie to the grave sites, Jane and I go to the church and Joe and Lois to St Agnes Girls College.'

'Well, they'd better be all back in their coffins when we get there,' said Auntie, 'that's all I can say.'

'We pick up our weapons tomorrow and we hit these places tomorrow night, not forgetting that Joe and Bruce also have their own weapons if we need more firepower.'

They picked up the weapons and went off to the pub for dinner.

Max said, 'Let's do a head count, or "dead count", if you like. First, there was Audrey and Alfred Campbell murdered in 1846. Now there's Stewart MacGregor missing with twenty-two girls, the bloke calling himself Joran, the two girls missing from here somewhere, the priest and the slutty looking female goon. Her supposed husband, Three Fingers , has been shot dead by the farmer, and the one who called himself Tick Tock has had his neck broken in the waterwheel. And has anyone noticed Paddy the grave digger hasn't been seen since the first day we meet him?'

But tonight, they were sure they would solve some of the mystery surrounding the Campbell family history that was a tangled mess with the Ryan and Anne Bonny clan, whoever they were.

Chapter Nineteen

Bruce and Auntie arrived at the graveyard gates. Auntie hated being here at night, not because she was frightened but because it didn't seem right disturbing those who were quietly sleeping below their feet. They couldn't help noticing, surrounded by a ghostly thin crescent of crystal grey, the moon in its rightful place in the sky, a constant reminder that she is the creator of the times and tides, songs and words of love, and regularly gives her support to young lovers. She is truly the mother of the sky, and she had the support of a million stars in the background. Occasionally, Auntie caught a glimpse of a twinkle as one winked at her, and the moon continued to cast its light over the tombstones in the graveyard, creating shadows that were easily imagined as an image of something else. They could tell the occupants were all back where they should be by the gloomy vapouring mist of their spirits shimmering across the tops of the graves. The moon was certainly awake tonight and in a party mood.

However, they were here, and they had a job to do, so in they went. Set in the back corner were the oldest graves with long grass almost covering the entire grave. These graves were from the fourteenth and fifteenth centuries and the headstones were impossible to read, having been lashed by Mother Nature's harsh weather for hundreds of years.

There was someone up in that area. It looked like one of the nuns – too dark to get a good look. They moved quietly up that way using the headstones for cover, but when they got close enough to see the area clearly, there was no one there. They looked at each other.

'We did see someone, didn't we?' Auntie said.

'Absolutely,' Bruce said, 'and it looked like one of those nuns.'

'Well, if it was, where is she now? We couldn't both have imagined we saw someone, could we?'

They searched the whole graveyard and found nothing.

*

Max and Jane had arrived at the church. Everything looked dark and lonely. A path ran along the stone wall to where the dead would have been carried from the church to the burial site. Just outside the stone wall were magnificent elm trees that stretched their limbs over the wall, providing shade and acknowledging the dead as they passed by. The porch entrance into the church was constructed with strong metal-strapped oak, which sent the message you were about to enter the church . Once inside, the darkness failed to hide the magnificent craftsmanship, and as their eyes surveyed the room, it was hard to miss the stained oak beams high up that took your eyes to the stained glass carefully inserted into the narrow lancet windows. The church was full of the fresh smell of flowers from the failed Sunday service. The rows of pews that lead to the carved altar, with the date, 1763, cut into it, were of hardwood oak, and in those days, where you sat depended on your standing in the village. This lovely old church seemed to be silently whispering , *Come in. I am your safe haven. I am your cocoon and transition to a butterfly*.

The vestibule was tucked away at the back of the church. They put the light on and poked around, looking through old files and bits of paper with biblical scribble. Some of the loose papers fell off the desk on to the floor. When Jane picked them up, she saw what looked like blood on the floor and scuff marks like something or someone been dragged along the floor. They followed the drag marks and the drops of blood here and there, but the trail ran out after a couple of metres. The pulpit had been knocked over and not stood upright. As Max bent down to pick it up, he saw the two brass rings to lift the trapdoor.

'Well, what do we have here?' he said to Jane.

*

Joe and Lois were standing inside the rock wall of the girls finishing school which, long ago, was called the Reformatory for Roman Catholic Girls. Lois said the thought of what might have happened to young girls inside there in years gone by terrorised her. They banged the large rapper on the big oak doors and rang the bell.

A small square panel opened, and a voice said, 'Yes?'

They explained the purpose of their visit, and a female voice said, 'Please come back tomorrow. We are unable to see anyone at this hour. This is the time of our religious hours.'

'We will return sharp at 9 am tomorrow,' said Joe, then to Lois, 'This whole place in there is a den of suspicion.'

The next morning, at exactly 9 am, they were at the door

again, and this time they were welcomed in.

Joe said, 'Who is in charge of this girl's college?'

'The Mother Superior.'

Lois said, 'Then we would like to talk to her.'

The sister said, 'I'm sorry she is not available at the moment.

'Well, when will she be available?'

'I'm afraid she will never be available, 'said the nun, 'We discovered her in the bedroom with her crucifix buried in her neck, and I'm afraid she is dead.'

'Christ! Bodies dropping like flies,' said Joe, 'Oops ... sorry, Sister.'

'Under the circumstances, my son,' she said, 'you are excused.'

*

Johno, Harrigan, and the Spiders were all together again at the pub, which had become their meeting place.

Joe said, 'We have narrowed it down to a triangle of the church, the graveyard and the girl's college. There's a lot more going on in those places than we were first aware of, and it's all bad. I think we should all stick together now.'

*

'What are you doing, coming out of the Mother Superior's room?' said Sister Mary.

The nun said, 'None of your business.'

Sister Mary said, 'I have been watching you lately and you've been missing at night. I wouldn't be surprised if you were a ring-in, somehow. You are very shaky on procedures you should know off by heart.'

*

When the Spiders arrived at the church, one bell was ringing spasmodically. They went into the belltower to find Sister Mary hanging from one of the bell ropes.

Joe said, 'We'd better find out who's doing this, or we will be next!'

After the police interviews and statements, they decided they would all go back to the graveyard.

Lois said, 'You know, whoever is doing this will have to have an accomplice who is helping them.'

At the graveyard gate, Auntie said, 'See up there in the top corner? That's where all the old graves are, and that's where we thought we saw a nun, someone in black, who just disappeared.'

'Okay,' said Max, 'let's all trundle up there and have a good look.'

It wasn't dark yet so they got a good look around. The long grass around one of the graves inside a wrought iron fence looked like it had been trampled down by small animals, but that was very unlikely. On closer examination, they could see where the fence around the grave had been carefully cut to remove and replace on demand. Not to be outdone, Max got down on his hands and knees and discovered that the top slab of the grave was actually hollow, made of some sort of light timber and covered with white shiny plastic to look like concrete. Down low on the front of what they now knew was a lid was a catch, very cunningly concealed in the long grass and under a lip. Joe opened the catch, and the lid came up on two struts, exposing steps going down into the unknown.

Chapter Twenty

The *Mary Jane* docked in Germany on schedule. The girls were loaded back on the bus to be transported to a large German disbanded convent where they would be split up into pairs, sold and placed in convents around the world as "servants of God". The gold bars were also stored at the convent awaiting further instructions from The Syndicate. Once the girls were sorted into pairs, they were placed in cell-like rooms with bars on the front.

Alice and Meg had been placed together and as luck happened, they had also been roommates back at the girl's school.

Meg said, 'They've shoved us into a concrete box, just four walls and two thin mattresses on the two bunks. The only light that will come in is from that small barred window, high up near the ceiling. There's a musty smell that is coming from the damp concrete floor, which the leak in the bottom of that toilet has contributed to over many years.'

The outside of the building wasn't much better it looked like it had lost its soul, grass and weeds growing up through the bricks and boards near the ground, and with cobweb covered windows, the whole place looked like it had just given up with the struggles and pain it had endured over centuries of life.

They had little sleep that night, being kept awake by the moaning of the timber trying to support the weight of the sagging roof and the sound of scurrying feet as small critters went about their night activity. Their concerns weren't the cell-like rooms but the open rows of showers in the morning with these apes, their guards, staring at their naked bodies. If one of them needed to go to the toilet, one girl would stand at the bars and warn the other if someone was coming or she would be caught with her pants down on the toilet.

A voice came over a loudspeaker. 'Attention, girls, you will be kept here until the British government or your parents pay the ransom money, 2.5 million pounds per child, in three weeks' time. If the money has not been paid, you will be sold to various places around the globe. Enjoy your stay.'

Their plan was certainly different to that: they planned to sell the girls even if the ransoms were paid.

The man who stood before Alice and Meg was a mean looking fellow. His teeth looked like the top of an old brick wall with bricks missing here and there, or the broken jagged glass on top of a jail wall. His jaw jutted out like a veranda over his neck and his bent nose had been broken several times . He had cauliflower ears, like those of a wrestler. His shirt was badly stained along with his suit, and the hair that he did have sat on his head like a felt pad. His breath smelt like a hairy gorilla's armpit. He was a slob.

He said, 'You two are the lucky ones. You will be allocated to someone here in Germany regardless of the outcome, but I can make your stay here more comfortable in return for some kind on your part.'

The two girls spat on the ground and turned away.

*

The parents who could afford to pay wanted to pay straightaway. The police advised against it. The odds of not getting their child back after the ransom was paid were too high.

'We need a lot more information and bargaining power than what we have,' said the police.

Chapter Twenty-One

The Spiders headed on down the rough-cut stairs into the crypt. The whole underground area was a maze of passageways, tunnels and rooms.

'Jesus,' Max said, 'this place is unbelievable! Christ knows what's down here, or for that matter, who.'

They lit some of the kerosene lamps on the walls along the way to save their torch batteries. Most rooms were family crypt rooms with four or five metal caskets in each, and there were carved shelves in the walls with long ago burnt down candles and shrivelled dead flowers that had been left by friends, who by now were most likely dead themselves.

Lois said, 'We need to check the names on all these caskets against our list of missing people. Joe and I will take the side rooms to the left.'

Jane said, 'Max and I will do the right-hand rooms. Bruce and Auntie can do the caskets on the shelves cut into the walls.'

Everyone agreed, so back to the start they went.

They had done seven or eight rooms when Jane said, 'Did anyone else hear that? Quiet! Listen, someone is calling out, but it's very muffled. It's further up the passage.'

They kept walking towards the sound, and then it stopped.

Lois called out, 'Is there somebody there? Keep calling out and we will find you.'

'Over here, over here,' came the reply.

They went into a large underground room with eight metal caskets with holes in them.

'They are viewing caskets,' said Auntie.

They opened the casket the noise was coming from.

'Jesus, who are you? they said.

She told them her name was Rosie, 'and would you please open that one there?'

They opened the casket. Hanna was unconscious due to the lack of sufficient air over the last two weeks.

'She still has a good complexion,' said Jane. 'We might not be too late.'

They gave her CPR, and she came to. Both girls were lucky to be found before it was too late. Any longer without fluids would have been a different story.

The Spiders opened the caskets one by one. They were shocked at what they found: Sister Margarita, who was supposed to have gone home sick, and had been replaced by a new nun; Liam Finnigan, the original graveyard maintenance man who had gone missing and had been replaced by Paddy O'Flarity; Joran, whom the police knew all about but no one else did, who was in fact ASIS, Australian Secret Intelligence Service; Paddy O'Flarity, the current graveyard maintenance man who had been reported missing some weeks ago; Three Fingers, who'd disappeared after he was shot by the farmer near Anne Bonny's grave; Dolly; and Frederick Hardwick, the priest who'd failed to turn up for the church service last Sunday.

'Now it's time to go find the culprit,' said the Spiders.

'So who put you in here?' said Bruce.

'Sister Ignatius,' the girls said.

'Why did she do that?' Bruce said.

The girls explained they were down there having a smoke when they'd found these caskets. They' opened the one with the nun in it, 'and Sister Ignatius came in and told us who the nun was in the casket, and she had replaced her but she said, "I'm not a real nun", she said. She was working for someone called The Syndicate, and then she shoved us in these steel caskets. So, what happens now?' the girls asked.

The Spiders told them about the other girls, who were missing, and that they would be taken to the police station and a plan organised for them to fly home.

And then the fun would start.

Spider, spider on the wall, how is it you never fall?

Chapter Twenty-Two

Sister Ignatius heard they had found the girls, and she knew they would be coming for her. There was never any help from The Syndicate after a failed operation, but she, of course, didn't see it that way. She had achieved her aim by hiding money and jewels that were the sins of God, that divided society into classes and promoted misery for many others. That was her thinking, not The Syndicate's, that was expecting delivery of the booty. It had come at a large price and loss of life, but so be it. She was a cold-hearted killer. *So what?* she said to herself. *Nothing comes free in this world.*

She had more work to do, and that work would be in Germany. She took what she needed in money from the casket, stripped off the black outfit she hated but had been forced to wear, and once again took up her Syndicate name, Zilla, and booked a flight to Germany. She was a middle order player in The Syndicate system because when she arrived at the old convent in Germany, most of the goons called her Ma'am and the one or two who were of the same standing as her called her Zilla.

*

Back at Hambleden, Harrigan had used his muscle and obtained approval for every casket in the underground crypt to be opened and names and contents logged. The military had been brought in for this task from London.

Harrigan said to the Spiders, 'I couldn't begin to tell you what was found. Hundreds of years of questions have been answered.'

Max said, 'Jane and I are going to talk to the two nuns left at the college tomorrow to see if we can get a lead on Ignatius, or whatever her real name is.'

Chapter Twenty-Three

They met the two nuns at the big oak doors of the girls school convent. Anyone could see they were in shock over the whole thing.

They said, 'If it's any help, we heard her booking a flight to Germany and then talking to someone, saying, "Yes, sir, no, sir. I have booked my flight. The girls have been sold. Are the girls and the gold safe?" We weren't game to interfere. We were going to the police tomorrow when she had gone and it was safe.'

Max passed this on to Harrigan, who simply said, 'Do the Spiders want to go?'

Lois, who would have normally have said no, said, 'If it wasn't for those poor girls in the hands of those bastards ...! If there is something we can do to help get them back, I'm in.'

Everyone stared at her in disbelief.

They said, 'Well, one in, all in, we guess.'

'Go then and do what you do best, but bloody well all come back. The government will, of course, reimburse your expenses. I will notify the German authorities who will issue you with weapons and any support you will require. I don't want you to go if you're not all happy to go.'

'No, we will all go,' said Jane. Everyone nodded in agreement. 'But before we go, we need to go to London to learn what ships were at the Port of London at the time the girls disappeared. They would need to go by ship as the gold would weigh several tons, and I'm betting the bus went along for the ride as well.'

They checked at the Harbour Master's Office, and sure enough, a merchant sailing vessel called the *Mary Jane* had left the port at about the same time the girls went missing.

'And guess what?' the Harbour Master said. 'There was a blue and white bus on the top deck, and she was bound for Germany.'

Now they could book a flight, as they knew where they were going.

*

At the old abandoned convent in Germany, the guy with the teeth like the top of a broken brick wall said, 'You two and the ones in the next cell are on your way now to your new home.'

Meg said, 'And where would that be?'

'It's a monastery in the mountains. That's all you need to know.'

After he had gone, Alice called out to the girls in the next cell, 'They are taking Meg and me to a monastery somewhere here in the mountains.'

'Okay,' the girls in the next-door cell said.

*

When Meg and Alice arrived at the foot of the Holy

Mountain in the Bavarian Alps, there were two men and a woman waiting with donkeys. The donkeys were small and had greasy thick fur and large ears, so they weren't pretty to look at. They weren't as smart as dogs or horses, but they were not dumb animals like some people said. As the girls began their way up the mountain, they could see the monastery half hidden in the mist and clouds. The trip would take three days.

They had only been going for a couple of hours, but their thighs were already aching, and they kept asking themselves what they had done wrong to be here and being transported up the mountain and into the clouds by these two small and uncomfortable donkeys. The huge mountain ahead of them was showing its power and strength, with Mother Nature helping with a wind that whistled an eerie message that the mountain was afraid of no man or beast. Higher up on the sloped peaks, the last of the snow was melting away by the last rays of the sun and gave it all an orange and yellow tinge. This was Bavaria's Holy Mountain. They looked up at it, and their hearts skipped a beat and sent shivers down their spine. They hoped it was only a dream and that they would wake up soon. As they got higher, the plants and shrubs were shorter as a fight against the wind, and even higher was mainly just gravel and stone. Nearing the end of the second day's climb, if they looked carefully, they could see whispers of water quietly and gently running down a moss-covered rock here and there on the high side of the track.

The woman said, 'We will be at the waterfall by nightfall.'

After another uncomfortable and restless night, kept awake by the roaring and rumbling of the water coming over the cliff from a great height, they woke to a bright sunny morning, but the wind was cold. The water came sliding over the well-worn rocks that seemed to be perfectly placed to create the best effect of the fall and speed of the water, with the sun producing rainbow colours in the spray just above the water's surface. As the sun hit the water on its way down to a rock pool, the colour of the water changed from light to dark blue, and a vortex was made by the funnel of water spiralling down from above into the rock pool, sending a pleasant cool spray into the air above and around the rock pool, with the ever-present little grebes frolicking in the spray.

On the last day of the climb, the rocky trail got narrower and slippery. On several occasions, the donkeys lost their footing and sent loose stones over the edges, spiralling down hundreds of feet to the ground.

As they got nearer the monastery, they got their first good look at it. The monastery had a very high stone wall around the buildings and Alice wondered if it was to keep people out or to keep the monks in. Really, the only thing she could see was the clerestory windows with stained glass high up near the roof line. There were quite a lot of buildings, and the woman told them there would be a church for prayer, a dormitory for sleeping, a cloister for meditation, a library for borrowing books, a balneary for bathing, infirmary for the sick, a chapter house for meetings and a refectory dining hall. She said the monastery was run by an abbot who oversaw the day-to-day running and finances. He was known as the father, teacher and the ruler of monks.

Chapter Twenty-Four

The Spiders were staying in Berlin in the suburb of Charlottenburg at the Hotel Indigo, and had made reservations at Crackers for the evening meal where they all had the warm brioche bread, Joe and Max had octopus, Bruce had rinderfilet, Lois had brook trout, Auntie had steak tartare and Jane had risotto. They all had the blueberry shortcrust with yoghurt and olive oil, and a port or cocktail to finish the evening. They all agreed they would meet at breakfast to discuss the next move. Breakfast hadn't changed in the years since they had been in Germany: fresh crusty or toasted bread rolls, cold cuts of ham or liver sausages, cheese and eggs how you liked them.

Now it was time to switch on the brain matter, and after talking about their plan, see the authorities for weapons and talk about any help they may have to give them.

Max said, 'Joe, go get us a suitable vehicle.'

They made some phone calls to Germany's Federal Intelligence Service and the Berlin police, who both knew they had arrived and where they were staying.

Lois said, 'So, they already know we're here and where we are staying. If they're that bloody smart, why haven't they found the girls yet? We should sneak off and stay somewhere else, pay cash, show them how smart we are.'

'I don't think we should piss these people off. We just might need them down the line,' Bruce said.

Joe arrived back with a Volkswagen people mover. They piled in and headed off to pick up their weapons. They were told by the police superintendent that if they found the girls, they were to stand down and contact the police.

Max told him, 'Pig's arse, we will! We have come here to get the girls, and when we find them – and we will – we won't be hanging around waiting for you, who have done absolutely nothing. And whether you like that or not, we're going up the guts with tons of smoke to find them. So, when you get there, bring body bags.'

That really pissed the superintendent off. *Bloody Australians rude bastards!* he thought as he went higher up the police authority ladder, but he was told they were to have a free hand, and heads would roll if anyone interfered. Now he realised these people obviously weren't just anyone, but Jesus, they were old! However, he would have to toe the line, "the heads would roll" part meaning his head as well. But he would only do what he had to do, and no more.

Joe was their escape man and had saved the day on many occasions in the past. He had gone shopping again for the supplies. When he returned, he showed he had been very busy. Neatly packed in the back of the van were several items: a roll of thin nylon rope, a small strong electromagnetic hook and cable with demagnetiser control, a mini Hot Devil oxyacetylene cutting torch, six cigarette lighters, three pairs of small and three pairs of medium rigger gloves, a high-powered gas canister arrow gun that fired an arrow half the length of a normal one and six arrows, four stun grenades, four door breaching explosives, six hand grenades and fifty extra rounds of ammunition for each of the weapons they carried. These escape and defence items might never be used but would stay in the vehicle under the 7Ps rule: prior preparation and planning prevents piss poor performance.

They went to the Crayfish Cave for the evening meal and shared what was called a table net for six . It was magnificent – drunken abalone, three dozen oysters, three dozen mussels, six half crayfish, prawn spring rolls, six pieces of barramundi, six pieces of King George whiting and one dozen split grilled prawns, served with a cold salad. And because the government was reimbursing the costs, they all had large margaritas. The Crayfish Cave didn't close till midnight, so they used the time to talk about the mission.

Max said, 'So, what do we know? Anyone, feel free to jump in if I miss something. Facts first. The girls came from good families for their legitimate ladies training, and they started their training, no problems.'

Everyone agreed so far. 'Yes,' they said.

'A woman sent from The Syndicate murdered Sister Margarita and took her place. She was sent to find the pirates' jewellery stash, and she did find some of it after murdering several people and hiding the money and jewels in caskets which have now been found. And that, my friends, the Spiders, will really upset The Syndicate. Don't be surprised if they haven't already sent someone to rectify that. Are we all okay so far?

'Now, here's a supposition. The woman pretending to be a nun calling herself Sister Ignatius knew the gold bars were being held in London awaiting transport out on the *Mary*

Jane. She organised the girl's dinner to coincide with the movement of gold, and The Syndicate was arranging the sale of the girls, and so they were spoken for and the money for each of them paid. What The Syndicate doesn't know is I think this so-called nun has a few more cards up her sleeve yet. And I think, because this has all been convent oriented from the start, that's where we should be looking. This is all to do with money, and nothing to do with medieval or biblical history.'

They agreed that Joe and Lois would check for convents and monasteries in Berlin. Bruce and Auntie would check when the sailing vessel, the *Mary Jane*, had docked, and Max and Jane would try and get the bus's movements after the ship had docked.

Bruce and Auntie, in the Harbour Master's Office, learnt the ship had docked two weeks ago and had now left for its return to London.

The Harbour Master said, 'Mind you, the bus didn't leave. It was driven off with a bunch of girls. It was one of those Nissan Civilian buses, blue and white.'

Max and Jane had nothing to add. Once the bus had left the port of Hamburg, who knew where it had gone.

Joe and Lois were at the State Library checking monasteries either closed or operational. There were no convents as such. It seems the usual rule was nuns were in convents and monks were in monasteries and there were sixteen of them over a 500 kilometre area.

'Jesus,' Joe said, 'It's going to take a month, and I don't think the girls would still be together by then. I don't think we have that much time.'

'We need more transport,' said Lois.

'Right,' said Max. 'Joe and Bruce, disappear from here and return with two more vehicles, and we'll work in pairs.'

They returned with two small Volkswagen vehicles. It was time to pack for a journey that could save twenty-two young girls.

Chapter Twenty-Five

Four of the girls were loaded into a motorhome and given a sleeping injection for the twelve-hour journey to Switzerland. There would be no problems crossing over. Germany was going to set up temporary border checkpoints to limit irregular migration and enhance internal security, but this hadn't happened yet, so they could drive straight through.

The girls were awake now and had been taken to a small alcove at the base of the Swiss Alps. Looking up, they saw what could only be explained as a "magic mountain", lifted from the pages of a travel magazine. The sides of the mountain reminded them of a heartbeat graph, or ECG as it's called, with its peaks and ridges, highs and lows. This mountain was surely the heart of the earth, sharing its pulse with everything around it. Behind them were the coloured domes of the township with its churches and cathedrals. Charles Dickens said Switzerland was where you changed your horse, and in the mountains, you took a deep breath of fresh clean air. The alpine lakes and grassy valleys went hand in hand with this magic mountain.

The only way up to the monastery was by a large cane basket operated by an old Ford engine pulley on a gantry that hung out over the cliff face at the top of the mountain where the monastery gate house entry was located. There was a phone in a box in the alcove, and after a call was made, the basket was released and started down. The girls were put into the basket along with food and supplies that would normally have gone by helicopter, but only a small amount had been requested, so it was going up with the girls. The basket began its return journey to the top.

When the basket arrived at the monastery, there were three monks waiting. One was particularly fat, or to be more polite, he was "rounder" than the others. They all had strange looking haircuts: either no hair at all or a sort of doughnut cut, hair with a hole in the middle (in other words, a tonsure). The four girls were helped out of the basket by the monks.

In thick but soft voices, they said, 'Welcome to heaven on earth, ladies.'

They were taken to see the abbot who told them they would now have new names.'

'We don't want new names,' they said. 'We have been abducted and brought here against our wishes.'

'No, my dears,' he said, 'you have been brought here for your own protection from those bad people that wish to harm you. No one can hurt you up here. We are giving you biblical names to fit in here for your stay, but you will have to earn your keep. You will all be working in the laundry.' As he pointed, he said, 'You are Lydia, you are Jemima, you are Naomi, and you, little one, will be called Hope. Amani and Axelle will show you around, and where you will sleep. They will be your keepers and advisers while you are learning the ways of God.'

The showing around part was simple: 'This is the laundry. You start at 6 am and finish at 6 pm. This is where you eat when the bell rings, and this is where you sleep.'

Lydia said, 'Jesus, do you think we are ever going to be found?'

'I know my father,' Jemima said. 'He is a determined bastard. He will have people out looking as we speak, and he will have threatened the government with all sorts of things. Yes, we will be found. The question is, how old we will be when they do?'

'I think the smart ones like ASIS, ASIO and MI6 will be looking for a common denominator to get us *all* back, not just you and me. I'll give you an example. Fishermen found that where warm water meets cold is where big fish and little fish gathered, and where big fish eat little fish. So, that's where they fished, to get them all, big and small, at the same time. So, you see, they're looking for the opportunity to get us all. They also want that gold back we saw on the boat.'

Yes,' said Jemima, 'you're right. I think our people will be much smarter than the dumb bastards that took us. They will also be better looking than that smelly one with the broken teeth!'

*

The rest of the girls were being grouped into lots of four as well for moving on to their destination. They were being kept roughly in their groups from the convent at Hambleden. Four were going to Denmark, four to Switzerland, four to Austria, four to France and four to Belgium. They would be travelling next week in motorhomes where they could all be put to sleep for the journey and border crossings.

As Germany shares its borders with nine countries, The Syndicate expected to get the girls across easily – or so they thought.

Chapter Twenty-Six

The power branch of The Syndicate was fuming at the loss of millions of dollars' worth of jewels and coins at the hands of Zilla, one of their own agents. The head operative in Germany had been instructed to find a contract Syndicate killer or killers, as he saw fit, to deal with Zilla as soon as possible. London was only one hour and forty minutes' flying time to Berlin, so a man by the name of Chuck would be flying in to meet up with a Sophia Schwartz at Brandenburg Airport, or as it's called by the locals, the Willy Brandt. The woman was German and therefore could speak the language, which would be a plus for their mission, because as far as Chuck went, he probably couldn't even spell "Germany". He was "bottom of the chain" scum. Sophia was a bit more upmarket, and although a cold killer, she could fit in and look the part at any level of society, and she might need to if she was to find the gold. Moving it was another problem; there were a hundred gold ingots on a pallet weighing around twelve tonnes. The Syndicate knew exactly where the gold and the girls were, and they had passed that on to Sophia and her cannon fodder sidekick, who were now on their way to the old convent.

*

The Spiders were at their third convent and monastery in three days, and they were running out of time. If they were right, the girls were going to be moved to different locations. Joe and Lois were approaching their fourth convent. It certainly looked like nobody owned it, but the intriguing part was the number of black cars and vans that were parked there. They rang the others to join them.

'This could be the place,' they said.

While they were waiting for the others, four motorhomes pulled up and the drivers went inside.

Joe said, 'I don't like the look of all this.'

He lifted up the bonnets, removed the rotor buttons from all the distributors and threw them away. They had just got back into the Volkswagen when a white Mercedes pulled up and a man and a woman got out. They drew their weapons and went in through the old gate house.

'Who the hell are they?' Lois said.

'Who knows?' said Joe, but they're not on our side. Whoever the bloke is, he could get the lead role in the Munsters, and she's one of those jubbly jugglers.'

The others arrived and Joe handed out the equipment. Joe kept the oxy torch and the stun grenades and gave Max the magnetic hook plate and rope and two door breaching explosives. Auntie had the coil of nylon rope, Bruce had the other two door breaching explosives, Lois had the arrow gun and Jane was back up with the 7.62 long range rifle with telescopic sights and a laser beam obtained from the police. Everyone had a lighter for the oxy torch, gloves and their extra ammunition.

'It's two storeys high,' said Max, 'but I'm betting everything will be happening on the ground floor. Maybe they have some bedrooms upstairs, but there shouldn't be anyone up there at this time of day. So do we all agree that we go in from the top?'

'Absolutely,' they all said.'

'Well,' Bruce said, 'let's get up there and find a way in.'

Chapter Twenty-Seven

Up high in the middle of the domed ceiling of the great hall was a large cathedral window that let daylight in. The years and harsh weather had weakened its structure, and it had been repaired and reinforced with a large steel plate to keep the massive weight of glass intact. The dome was made of ten large individual glass frames. The Spiders picked the one where the putty was cracked and with more than half missing. It would be the easiest one to remove the glass from, leaving a nice square-framed hole.

They used the magnetic plate and gave the small hook, the size of a hand, to Lois to carry, which she hooked into her belt. Max attached the magnetic plate to the large reinforced steel plate on the dome's structure and slid down the cable as far as the second floor. Because he was the first one, he had to keep swinging backwards and forwards to get onto the upstairs walkway that ran along the left-hand side of the building. Then he tied the end of the cable to the walkway railing so the others could slide straight onto the upstairs landing of the walkway that ran along past the rooms. The walkway had a safety rail or wall they could look over down to the great hall, so they would be able to see and hear any action that occurred down there, and more importantly, anyone coming upstairs.

When all the Spiders were on the walkway, they demagnetised the plate and it came spiralling down to where they were. They attached the plate to the steel railing of the walkway and coiled the cord up on the floor by the rail. There was an identical open walkway opposite the one they were standing on, and more rooms; they couldn't get there from where they were standing. There was a separate set of stairs on the other side of the great hall. Both walkways ran to a dead end at the last room.

A man came running in through the great hall yelling out, 'Zilla!' They looked over the rail and there she was – the fictitious Sister Ignatius, also known as Zilla.

The man was yelling, 'The motorhomes won't start!'

'What? None of them?'

'None of them!'

'Well, at least we got four girls off to Switzerland yesterday,' said Zilla.

'Bugger!' said Max, who overheard the conversation, 'We're too late for four of them. If I remember, it's a twelve-hour trip from Berlin to Switzerland so they will be there by now. When we get out of here, we'll ask Harrigan to get all the motorhomes in that area checked, but I think we are too late.'

The Spiders now saw the sewer rat Syndicate killer, who Joe and Lois had seen getting out of the car outside, on the opposite walkway about to shoot Zilla. But they needed her alive for information about the girls. The Spiders weren't ready to be found yet, so no gunfire. Lois poked an arrow into the gas canister gun and without a sound, shot him through the neck.

The motorhome driver was joined by the other drivers who all went outside to try and fix their vehicles. They checked the spark plug leads into the distributor cap and one of them saw the rotor button was gone. The others then checked theirs and they found the same result: rotor button missing. The drivers spoke to Zilla and the other Syndicate members, all contracted killers at various skill levels but all expendable. Zilla was obviously the senior operative; when she spoke, they jumped.

'There are people here who shouldn't be,' she said. 'Spread out, inside and outside, and bring them to me.'

Max said, 'I think we should move to the last room on the walkway. That way we can't be attacked from both sides at once. We'll only have to defend ourselves one way.'

Inside the bedroom of the last room was a window with four steel bars.

Max said, 'Bring the bed over to the window and cut those bars off with the oxy torch. Tie the nylon rope that Auntie's got onto the bed. Out you go, Joe, with Lois, and we'll pass your weapons down. We want some back-up coming in from behind them. Be very careful; they have people outside looking for us as well as that woman, whoever she is. She won't be on our side.'

Lois went out first, followed by Joe, and their weapons were passed down. They could hear voices coming from around the corner of the building: 'If anything happens to these girls, Victor, it's the death penalty for all those concerned. We will all be hung, you know that, don't you, Victor?'

They turned the corner — and they were both suddenly dead.

'I thought we were finished with killing people,' Lois said.

'We're only killing the bad ones, Lois,' Joe said, 'and that's two less.'

When they got around the front of the building, the four motorhome drivers were leaning against the side off a motorhome, smoking. Joe climbed on to the roof, leaned over and dropped a stun grenade among them. They staggered around, holding their ears, and their noses were bleeding.

Joe slid off the roof and slit their throats. He said to himself, *Jesus, if you live to be old, you'll regret it. Years ago, I would have jumped down.*

'It's all clear out here,' Lois called out.

They went in through the big oak doors into the great hall and worked their way around close to the wall. Three men saw them. There was a large statue of Jesus with Mary which they hid behind. The men opened fire. The one with the machine gun opened up with rapid fire and blew Jesus' head clean off. As the statues were blown apart, they were getting smaller and Joe and Lois had nowhere to go. Up on the second floor walkway, the Spiders heard the shooting, came out of the room, looked over the rail into the great hall, saw Joe and Lois trapped behind what was left of the statue and fired. The three goons had no idea who was shooting or where it was coming from, and they were shot to pieces.

'That's nine of them gone now,' Lois said. 'How many of these goons are here, for Christ's sake?'

Joe and Lois were joined downstairs by Auntie and were moving towards several rooms under the opposite walkway to the Spiders, who were watching their moves. Two men and a woman came out of a room behind them.

'Hands on the back of your heads,' they said.

'Who the hell are you?' Auntie said. 'We're from the taxation department, and we're here to help.'

'Bullshit!' said the woman. 'You're going to be dead in a minute, so who are you?'

Max was watching all this unfold. He said they couldn't risk a shot; they were too close together. The magnetic plate was still attached to the steel rail. With the coil of the rope, he swung down and knocked them arse over. Auntie was first to her feet and shot the woman through her earhole. Joe got the other two.

Bruce called out from the walkway, 'I see you're still shooting people in different parts of the body. Once again, I can't wait to see where you hit next.'

Chapter Twenty-Eight

The girls were all in one cell with Zilla in a stand-off with Sophia outside the cell.

'I have been sent here to kill you. You are a stupid woman. The Syndicate trusted you to do as they instructed. You have betrayed their trust and the penalty for that is death.'

'Yes, so I understand,' Zilla said, as she slowly walked over to Sophia and shot her in the left eyeball as she thought, *Damn, I've really got to find out why I'm pulling my shots to the left.*

Zilla grabbed four girls at gunpoint and said, 'You're coming with me to Belgium.'

She took them out and into a black Volkswagen van. Bruce was outside checking the perimeter, and he saw the van drive off. Its number plate was FIGJAM; translated as "Fuck, I'm good; just ask me".

The twelve girls left in the cell were over the moon to see the Spiders. They said they knew where the others had gone: two to a mountain in Germany, four to a mountain in Switzerland, and four five minutes ago to somewhere in Belgium.

Max said, 'You young ladies have been through the wringer. You all have been very brave. The police will be here soon and take you to a hospital to get checked out, and then home. Oh, and Rosie and Hanna have been found and are safe and well.'

Max rang the police and told them all about what had happened and that there were twelve girls to go for check-ups. The Spiders were going to Switzerland and Belgium to find the other girls.

'And before I forget, tell the superintendent to bring ten body bags. And the gold is not here; it's been moved.'

The superintendent rang Lieutenant Commander Harrigan and said, 'Jesus, who are these people, sir?'

'They call themselves the Spiders,' Harrigan said. 'They're old but they're good, better than anyone you or I have at our disposal. I have found it's best to just let them run the race at their own pace. And ten body bags sound about average for them. The sad part is that one of these trips, one or some of them aren't going to come home, and that will break my heart. We are all very close friends. And when you get there today, don't be surprised if they have all gone.'

Chapter Twenty-Nine

The only monastery the Spiders hadn't checked yet was a monastery at the top of the Holy Mountain in the Bavarian Alps, 583 kilometres from Berlin where they were staying, a seven-hour trip, which is why it had been left till last. They had hoped the one they were looking for was closer.

They packed the van with their personal gear and the survival gear (the 7Ps), and they took one of the Volkswagens as well. They decided to leave in the afternoon and stay somewhere overnight close to the mountains for an early start next day in case this monastery was the one they were looking for. They stayed overnight in Bavaria and the restaurant they chose was magnificent with beautiful German food. Next morning, they headed off to the Holy Mountain. There was a place at the foot of the mountain that hired out donkey.

The lady said, 'It's the only way to get to the top unless you can fly or have a helicopter, and it's a three-day journey.'

Max said, 'How long ago is it since anyone has visited the monastery?'

'A few weeks ago. A woman hired four donkeys and said she had stores to take up to the monastery, but that was a lie, as they fly everything by chopper these days. She said she needed to take them away to load. She paid, left and returned the donkeys a week later.'

'We will need seven donkeys,' Max said.

'They will be ready in one hour.'

The donkeys they rode carried their weapons and some personal gear, the last donkey carrying their camping gear and supplies like food and water. The sun was just making its way through the clouds and when it found a gap, it filtered its warmth through the mountain's canopy, smiling on the birds and critters that lived there. They could just make out the high steeple on top of the monastery's roof through the mist and the cloud. The air was fresh and crisp as the donkeys plodded their way up the zigzagging track, making hard work of it. The large rocks lying silently on each side of the track were slowly carving their story into the landscape. The pack donkey at the rear was a pain in the arse, pulling and stopping, and upsetting the routine of the others that had developed into a reasonable pace.

On day two, they arrived at the waterfall. Even from down where they were, they could see the frothy bubbles as the water plunged over the slippery rocks cascading down to a large rock pool.

Lois said, 'Look how the landscape changes when there's an abundance of water. There's all sorts of plants, flowers and green velvet somewhere between moss and grass, and many colourful flowers, like Alpine roses – and here's the famous Bavarian edelweiss. It's a mountain flower that belongs to the sunflower family and thrives at high altitudes in rocky limestone. This is a perfect scene for a house and garden magazine or a travel brochure.'

They were now being shown the power and magic of

Mother Nature. Dragonflies, butterflies and tiny little dabchicks all frolicked in the rainbow mist of the fall.

Suddenly there was gunfire, bullets spitting into the rock pool, coming from somewhere up high. They all took cover wherever they could find it. Jane managed to get to her donkey and retrieve her rifle, and found a large rock for cover. She made herself comfortable behind the rock and used the scope on the rifle to scan the area at the top of the falls.

There you are, you bastard, she said to herself. She pulled the trigger and over the falls he fell, into the rock pool.

'Jesus,' Max said, 'it's a monk! Why would he want to shoot us?'

Two more shots went spitting into the pool. They all took cover behind the rock with Jane.

Max said, 'Well, we are sitting ducks down here while they have the high ground. They could keep us here as long as they want. Any ideas from anyone would be good.'

Bruce said, 'Normally, it's not good to split the fire power, but in this case, there's no choice. I think Lois, Joe and I should leave the donkeys here and go up the track behind them while Jane can keep them busy with the rifle and you can make sure they don't steal the donkeys. We don't know how many there are.'

They sent Auntie to guard the donkeys and Max and Jane kept watching the high ground, hoping for another shot. They didn't have an unlimited supply of ammunition. The three Spiders climbed up the side of the track till they were above and behind the waterfall on a small plateau where a narrow, fast running, deep creek fed the waterfall from who knows where. The current was very strong as it shot out over the edge of the well-worn slippery rocks and down to the pool at the bottom. They lowered themselves into a cavity in the side of the rocks next to where the water went slithering over the edge and waited.

They didn't have to wait long. A monk in a safety vest orange robe appeared. He was almost on top of them when Lois shot an arrow into his eye socket, another silent kill.

'Four arrows left,' she said.

'Save your arrows,' Bruce said. 'We'll shoot the next one that comes along.'

It wasn't long before they heard, 'Are you there, Harry?' Joe whistled quietly. As the monk came over, following the sound, Joe and Bruce both shot him.

'Well, now we know these people are not monks. I very much doubt they would have a name like Harry.'

Two more shots rang out from below. They looked over the edge. Max was waving them down. When they returned, they learnt the two shots were from Auntie, as a so-called monk met his maker with a bullet hole up through the nose and into the brain.

Bruce said, 'Well, you're narrowing down the new places you can hit someone. I can't wait for the next episode.'

Things became quiet for several hours, so they set up camp with a two-hourly changeover and roving picket just in case.

The morning was dull, drab and cold for the last day's climb, and they now knew there would be a shit fight when they got there. These people were no more monks than Max was a gynaecologist. They had shortened the odds by four, but how many more were there? Looking at the size of the place, from what they could see, there would be at least another dozen, Max thought. They needed somehow to avoid a gun fight at the "OK monastery Corral" and get away with the girls scot-free.

Chapter Thirty

The Spiders arrived at the top and found somewhere to hide in what looked like a large storm water drain.

Bruce, being the plumber, said, 'This large man-sized drain tells me part of this monastery is underground, and that, my friends, the Spiders, is good news for us. These sorts of half-in and half-out buildings on mountains with the ground sloping away, like this one, must have a ground seepage drain. In the winter high up here, a huge amount of water hits the ground and seeps down around the bottom structure of the building, undermining the structure of walls and footings. This large drain we are standing in will run right around the underground part of the monastery to catch the ground water seepage. There will be a gigantic flushing tank and pump somewhere that will almost fill this drain during the flushing process. There have been cases where a house was pushed up by over a dozen centimetres by water under the foundation. Safety regulations insist on an escape route from the bottom part of the building, so the engineer will have put in a drain and made it big enough for an escape route as well. Somewhere along the drain will be two or three steps up to the entrance of the underground part of the monastery. There may even be two entrances along the drain.'

They synchronised their watches and agreed one of them should remain behind in case someone tried to block the drain and cut off their retreat with the girls, who presumably were there, but everything that had happened said they were there, all right.

'So,' Max said, 'who is staying at the entrance so we don't get trapped?'

Auntie said she would stay. She wasn't good in confined spaces, like the crypts at the graveyard. Max reminded them to put phones on buzz and stay in touch with message only.

'If you are really in the shit, ring and leave your phone on so we can hear what's going on.'

They all had torches, but to conserve the batteries, they were only using one. There were lights mounted high on the walls of the drain, and there would be a light switch at the door into the monastery, they said to themselves. They arrived at the entrance door but kept going to see where the drain went further on. Bruce was right – there was another entrance. And further on, the drain stopped at a set of stairs, going up to a trapdoor in the ceiling of the drain. They would need to look for both these exits when they got inside. There was also another large pipe coming into where they were standing.

Bruce said, 'That will be the flush pipe that goes to the tank and pump.'

They worked their way back to the first door entry from the drain. The door was locked from the inside, so Joe used one of his door breaching explosives and hoped there was no one in the underground section of the monastery. They entered what looked like a large room. They all turned off their torches and realised why no one was down here at that time of night. The room was full of planter boxes of marijuana. There must have been 500 plants, rigged up to twenty-four-hour lights.

Lois said, 'Well, the plot really thickens now, doesn't it? I wonder how many of these "monasteries" are around the world.'

Of course, this was not a monastery anymore; it had been taken over by The Syndicate.

'We need to get out of this bright light,' said Max, 'We need to maximise our rest time after the climb while all is quiet and dark.'

There were four rooms off the large growing room. The first was a chemistry laboratory, the second was a storage room for chemicals, the third room was full of Hazmat suits on hooks and the fourth were a set of rooms with decontamination showers and gowns.

'Jesus,' said Joe, 'this is a full-blown meth set-up. Anyone want to guess who's behind all this?'

'No,' they said. They already knew – it would be The Syndicate.

They camped out in the laboratory for the night, and each one quietly knew tomorrow would be a huge, dangerous day.

They woke to the sound of people going about their business above them.

Max said, 'We'd better get our arses out of here or we'll be trapped.'

As he spoke, a man and a woman in white coats came into the growing room and headed for the laboratory they were in.

'Bugger,' said Max, 'we don't want to kill people we don't have to, but these two aren't going to be in that category.'

When they came into the lab, Bruce grabbed one of Lois's arrows and pushed it in through the woman's neck, pulled it out, and handed it back to Lois, saying, 'Thanks.'

Joe did something simple: he just shot the bloke in the chest.

'Right,' Max said, 'get these bodies out into the drain, and let's get out of here.'

They sent Auntie a message and the answer came back: "All good this end".

They used the door the lab people had entered and found themselves in a passageway left and right with a set of stairs in front of them, so up they went. Now they were looking at what they knew as the great hall. A remarkably unconventional design compared to the last one they'd been in, this one was perfectly round with five openings and passages going off like the spokes of a wheel. The large oak front doors were directly in front of them that led to the gatehouse and the donkeys. They decided to do the passageways clockwise; they worked their way round the hall to the first opening and disappeared in. Ahead, somewhere down the passage, they could hear female voices.

It can't be that easy, Max thought.

'The voices are coming out of the next room,' said Lois.

In they went, guns drawn. There were four women in what was obviously the kitchen. They ranged in age from probably eighteen to forty years old, and they were terrified.

Joe said, 'Be quiet, ladies. We are here to get you out. What's your name?

'Sheree.'

'Find a pencil and paper and draw a map of this place as you know it, starting from here. Then carry on naturally. We will come back for you. Don't go away from here or we can't take you.'

Lois and Jane said, 'Where are the girls who just arrived?'

They said they would be in the laundry.

'Okay, hurry up with the map. Don't worry how rough it is; you're not going to be selling it.'

Max looked at the map and said, 'Left out of here twenty metres, a door to the other passage, turn left and the laundry is on the right. Let's go.'

The head honcho, calling himself the abbot, had been told the men sent to dispose of the strangers at the waterfall had been found dead, two lab workers were missing and there were seven donkeys tied up at the gatehouse.

'The bastards are here somewhere,' he said to his offsider, whom he called Costello. 'Make sure everyone is armed and alerted.'

They found the laundry and another four girls. Two had been there for more than five years; the other two were the ones they were looking for.

Max said, 'Where would I find the boss man here?'

Meg said, 'He is quite schizophrenic, and a pig of a man. You will find him at the end of the passage, in a large office marked on the door, "Abbot and Costello".'

Chapter Thirty-One

Meanwhile, the phone rang in the abbot's office at the monastery in the Swiss Alps. The four girls were going past and stopped outside to listen.

'Yes, sir, we are all systems go at our end for the delivery. It will be too heavy for the chopper for one trip, and we don't want to bring attention to ourselves with chopper trips back and forth. The basket will be the quiet and most secretive way to get the gold up here. It will take some time with ten bars at a time, but time is what we've got plenty of ... Yes, sir, we will let you know exactly when the movement will take place. We might even be able to sneak down in one of the gold trips in the empty basket.'

'These people aren't who they want us to think they are,' said Jemima. 'Real monks wouldn't be involved with smuggling gold bars. Well, I don't think they would, would they?'

*

Max said he would find the so-called abbot, and the rest of them were to round up the girls and women and he would meet them in the great hall.

Joe said, 'Do you girls know where the great hall is?'

They said they did.

'Right, go there and wait.'

Lois went with the girls, and Bruce and Joe went for the other girls in the kitchen.

The abbot was puffing a cigar and sipping a port when Max walked in.

'I wondered when we would meet,' he said, 'but I was hoping for the shoe to be on the other foot.'

Max said, 'You and The Syndicate's drug ring days have ended, along with the kidnapping of females put to work as captured slaves. You're going to be put away for a long time.'

A voice from behind said, 'I don't think so.'

Max turned, and Costello was pointing a gun at him. 'You're either very good or very lucky, and by the looks of your age, I'd say very lucky.'

'Then you'd be wrong,' Lois said, who had come back to see if Max was all right. Costello then had the best part of an arrow buried in the back of his head.

When they looked around, the abbot had gone out a side door. People were running everywhere, as there had been several shots fired. They worked their way back past several look-alike monks who threw their arms in the air and got out of the way. They arrived at the great hall where there were seventeen females waiting with Bruce and Jane.

'Quick!' said Max. 'Back downstairs through the growing room and out through the drain.'

On their way past the laboratory, Joe said, 'Just got to duck in here and leave a calling card.'

He started a fire in one corner near all the chemicals and hurried out and joined the others just as a siren started.

He said, 'What's the siren mean?'

Bruce said, 'It means we'd better hurry. They are flushing us out.'

They flicked the light switch, but no lights.

Bruce said, 'They go off when the flush pump starts. Let's get out of here before we all get soaked.'

The twenty-three of them headed off toward the opening.

Max said, 'We should already be seeing the light at the end of the tunnel, as they say.'

'Something is very wrong,' said Jane.

When they got to the drain entrance, a red light was flashing the words, "Tunnel Flooding Activated", and a steel door had come down and sealed the entrance. They were now up to their knees in water. Bruce fastened his last door breaching explosive to the steel door at the bottom, hoping that if it didn't blow the door open, it might make a hole for some of the water to drain away. They all stood back for the blast. It didn't blow the door but they could see where a small crack had started in the mechanical side of the door. Now they were up to their waist in water.

'Hurry up,' Joe said. 'These things don't work underwater.' Max had the last two explosives. 'Put the two of them on and pray.'

The water was now up to their shoulders. They turned their backs to the explosion, covered their ears and closed their mouths. *Boom!* went the double explosion, and now there was a large hole in the door. The two dead bodies they had left in the drain, that had washed down with the water, were lying against the steel door. The water dropped to their waist and would stay that way until the supply tank was empty.

The hole was big enough for one person to squeeze through, but there were steel bars on the other side that weren't there before. The water was streaming out through the bars. What shocked them was Auntie had been shot in both shoulders and was chained to the steel bars. Joe, being the skinniest, squeezed through the hole and cut two bars out with the portable oxy cutting torch, with just enough gas left to cut a third one out. As they were all coming out, Joe slid the chains over the cut bars to release Auntie. She was in a bad way and had lost a lot of blood.

'Where's that noise coming from?' said Jane, and as she spoke, an ex-military Bell UH-1 Iroquois (Huey) helicopter rose up over the cliff edge and started firing. They took cover behind the big blade of a Caterpillar D6 bulldozer.

'Jesus,' Max said, 'how did this get this up here? Must have used a "Sky Lifter" Chinook helicopter.'

'This must have been a scheduled drug pick-up,' Lois said, 'and we have run smack bang into it.'

Joe said, 'Can you fly that thing, Max?'

'No, no, he can't! He learns as he goes. We've been flying with him before–.' they all said.

'And I don't feel like shitting my pants again, and not while they're wet,' said Bruce.

'Yes, and I was a nervous wreck,' said Auntie.

'He's not that bad,' said Jane, 'and if we are all going to get out of here, there's no choice. We will just put on the big girl pants and fly with Max.'

Bruce jumped into the cabin and fired up the Caterpillar. He lifted its blade up to protect everyone from the bullets and drove towards the chopper. The pilot jumped out. He didn't want to be in it if it was squashed by the Caterpillar. The blades were still spinning; it only needed someone to fly it. Bruce backed the machine in close to the chopper and lifted the blade of the dozer to protect everyone getting in.

'I can only take eight at a time,' Max said. 'I'll come back for the rest, but first, as soon as I get airborne, I'll take care of these bastards.'

Two Spiders went with each trip. The first to go were Lois, Auntie and six girls. As they lifted off, there was a huge explosion and the whole monastery blew up.

'That's the calling card Joe left them,' Max said.

'Nice lift-off, Maxi baby,' said Lois, and Auntie was smiling.

Max banked around, opened fire with the chopper's guns and cut them to pieces. It was a rough landing, but no one cared as they were only two feet off the ground . Auntie was in a lot of pain, she had lost a lot of blood, and her skin was cold and clammy. Their phones were buggered from being underwater in the drain. Max said he would use the chopper's radio for an ambulance, and back up he went. He was only supposed to take eight but because it was all downhill and only a five-minute ride, he took another eight girls, Jane and Bruce plus himself. The last trip was for the last seven girls and Joe, who sat up with Max as copilot. As they lifted off, the abbot came out of the drain.

Max said, 'See that button there, Joe? That's for the guns. It's your privilege, mate.'

Max banked around and came down straight at the abbot, and Joe let him have it. When they got to the bottom, there were three ambulances, two police cars and Harrigan.

He smiled and said, 'I see you're still learning to fly, Max.'

Max said, 'Yes, sir. I suppose I'll get it right one day.'

Their vehicles were still there, and someone would need to get the donkeys. They told Harrigan they would stay there again that night, and they would be going to Switzerland tomorrow without Auntie.

Harrigan said, 'We will visit her in hospital and look after her till you get back ... and, Max, try not to get someone else shot, will you?'

Chapter Thirty-Two

During the evening meal, the Spiders discussed their options.

Jane said, 'There seems to be a thing about monasteries in the mountains. The Syndicate have realised the authorities leave them to themselves. It's all too hard to get way up in the mountains probably just to say hello, or they would need a search warrant and some hard evidence of a crime before a judge would even consider going into a monastery. So, they're left alone to their own resources. I think The Syndicate slowly move their people in, and over a period of several years, they replace the real monks with their own people. Just as people steal expensive cars to sell on the black market, there are people who trade in humans for undesirables like The Syndicate, and they pay big money for them, placing them in situations they can't escape from, like these monasteries we have seen. So, my advice would be to stick to monasteries high in the Alps.'

Everyone smiled and clapped.

Max said, 'Well-spoken, Jane, and we all agree. We will start tomorrow and check them out after a resupply of ammunition, four more door breaching explosives, two more stun grenades, and the rope we left behind. Lois has two more arrows left. They will be too hard to get at short notice, so she will have to use them sparingly.'

They lost a day while they went back for the other Volkswagen and the resupply. They spent the next three days visiting monasteries, but they all seemed above board and very professionally run. The one that interested them most was on top of the Cathedral Mountain in the Alps. They arrived in what the sign said was a viewing park of Cathedral Mountain and the Abbey of St Martin.

'Jesus,' they all said, 'we aren't going to try and climb that, are we?'

'Shit, no!' said Max, 'Look at it – sheer rock face and overhanging ledges.'

'I think you would have to fly up,' Joe said, 'We should have kept that chopper.'

'No good,' said Lois. 'They would know we were coming. Where does this dirt track go?'

The sign on the gate said, "No entry, private property" and the gate was padlocked. They all climbed over the gate and went for a walk around the base of the mountain. Where Bruce went to relieve himself behind some bushes, he saw a small track that went into an alcove. It looked a well-used area, off the ground near the side of the mountain that was a sheer wall all the way to the top. There was a metal box hidden in the bushes on a post. Printed on the box was, "Call for basket". They forced the small padlock open, and inside was a phone.

'Well, we now know how to get up there. We will need some sort of credentials, or they won't send the basket down. I think we need to talk to Harrigan for some official paperwork and business cards.'

Harrigan organised identification cards for them as part of the World Health Organisation on a goodwill tour, and he made an appointment for them. St Martin would send down their helicopter for them. It was a 5-seater JetRanger for four passengers and the pilot, so it would have to go back for the last two people. It was all arranged for tomorrow a 9 am pick-up at the local oval.

It wasn't the plan they wanted, so they changed their plan to suit. The plan now was to leave Max and Jane till last and Max would dispose of the pilot, strap him up in the copilot seat and fly back. He would land close to the others who would be waiting for him. He would land with his back to them, and with the dust and wind from the rotor blades, they would have to turn away, then he would flick the switches, get out with Jane and join them. Going back would be harder to deal with, and they decided to cross that bridge when the time came. They couldn't take their survival gear on this trip, but if things worked out all right, that would be going up in the basket.

They were all picked up on time the next day. When the pilot came back for Max and Jane, he realised the pilot was just a young bloke trying to make his way in the world. He didn't want to set the world on fire; he just wanted a ride to the top of life's hill, in other words, a fair go and a bit of hand. He knew nothing about St Martin's, he was just the chopper pilot for the abbey, and he was only on call. He and his chopper didn't live on the mountain. Max didn't want to kill this bloke for no reason.

'What's your name?' Max said.

'I'm Peter, and I live with my wife, Gabby, in the valley. Please don't kill me!'

'There will be no need for that,' Max said, 'but we will need your help.'

Max gave him all the information from the past, and together they formed a new friendship and a new plan. Peter said he always kept a sleeping bag in the chopper. Sometimes on a job, he would sleep on the chopper overnight, and Max was welcome to it when they executed the new plan. When they landed, Max lagged back from the main group with Joe and told him the plan; later, Joe would let the others know.

The Syndicate must have had to find a lot of little round fat men to fill the role, or these ones were the real McCoy. This so-called abbot was a picture-perfect double for the one Joe had riddled with bullets. *Where do they find these people?* Max thought. They were all very pleasant and gave them access to anywhere they wanted to go. Obviously, what they didn't want them to see was hidden away. They had a lunch of cold meat and salad, very basic but fresh. They probably had the lobster and altar wine for the evening meal after they had gone. Although none of them had ever been in a real monastery, it all looked ridgy-didge.

When Peter had the chopper beating the air into submission, they said thanks and goodbye to the abbot. When they were all in, the middle door was left open and Peter hovered the chopper over close to the bushes on the side where the open door was. Nobody could see with their backs to the chopper and bending over from dirt and shit that the chopper sucked up. Max jumped out with the sleeping bag and rolled into the bushes as the chopper spun around and lifted off.

On the ground, Peter said, 'Max and I have worked together on a new plan, and it has been agreed that one call from you people and I will come for you immediately.' They all said thank you, and they would see he was well compensated.

Peter had told Max the controls for the basket were through the trees at the cliff overhang, far enough away from the monastery not to hear the winch motor. When someone rang for the basket, it was answered in the monastery, and someone went out to the winch to operate it, but the muffled sound of the old Ford motor would not be heard, he said. The basket phone would not be used for obvious reasons. At exactly 9 am, Max would send the basket down and the Spiders would put all the survival gear in, and hopefully a couple of Spiders as well. When they were at the top, they would go into their black ops mode, and see if they had made a bad mistake, or if they were on the money.

Chapter Thirty-Three

Max had a reasonable night in the scrub as, to his amazement, the sleeping bag had small heating elements sewn into the lining of the bag and six AAA batteries with enough power to heat the bag for eight hours.

At 9 am, Max sent the basket down. There was no starter button; he had to use a crank handle to turn the motor over. They were surprised at how big the basket was. There was a cable coming from each corner of the basket, attached to one single cable through heavy-duty eyelets into a steel ring on the end of the single pulley cable. They were able to fit all the gear and Bruce and Jane into the basket. The cold mountain wind whistled through their hair and stung their ears and face as the basket swung its way to the top.

When they got there, Jane said, 'Shit! What a scary and dangerous ride that was, swinging side to side up the sheer rock side of the mountain. I'll take a ride with Max any day after that.'

*

The four girls, who had decided to go along with the bullshit names they had been given, knew something was going on. Apart from what they had learnt by listening to the abbot's phone call, something else was going on. Who were those old people there yesterday who they weren't supposed to see? They were old, but they looked super fit, like they could slit your throat and you'd still be smiling. But strangely, they looked like good people, and there was just something about them that gave them hope.

*

The Spiders were now gathered around the Ford winch motor, ready for the next move.

Max said, 'With Auntie in hospital, we're uneven, so Bruce, you go with Joe and Lois, and Jane comes with me. There's a side door that goes into the large kitchen we saw yesterday. You three go that way and Jane and I will go through the back door that we know goes through to the laundry. Stay in touch using message, with phone support on buzz.'

Max and Jane silently slid through the door into the laundry. There were two girls in there and a podgy monk who was pulling out his gun. He was far too slow – Jane shot him in the neck.

The girls threw their arms in the air and said with tears in their eyes, 'Please don't shoot us! We have been kidnapped and brought here. We only want to go home.'

'Do you know where the basket winch is?'

'Yes,' they said.

'Go and hide there till we come for you.'

The style of the kitchen they were now in was Western

European Gothic. The rose windows were divided by ornamental stonework called tracery which gave this large kitchen a cold and eerie look, a place for work and nothing else. This part of the monastery had been refurbished over time, but the kitchen had been spared in an effort to keep some form of the Gothic features that were prevalent in days gone by.

During their tour yesterday, they had asked what was behind the big wooden oak doors, with their panels held together with black steel battens bolted across the doors in a perfectly straight line. They were told that was the old part of the monastery, and nobody had been through those doors in years. Max had made a mental note: that's where the Spiders would definitely be going, and they had talked about it later at great length.

Max buzzed and left a message for the others that they had found two girls and sent them to the basket location to wait. Joe, Lois, and Bruce had found six girls, including twins, and had sent them to the basket location with the others.

'This monastery was all built above ground, so there will be no drain to drown in,' said Joe, 'so we need to be watching for a possible escape route just in case.'

*

The four girls knew something was happening. They were nosing around in the Abbot's office. Lydia was in the passageway keeping watch when three men she'd had never seen before came in from a side door.

'I didn't like the look of these girls when they arrived. Where's the other one?' they said.

'Naomi said it's her birthday today, so she's gone home for her party.'

'Keep your smart mouth shut,' the one with the strange teardrop mouth said to her, 'and take these three downstairs,' he said to the other two goons.

Lydia followed them till they disappeared through a self-locking door and they were gone. She would have to find another way.

*

Over a loudspeaker was heard, 'There are intruders in the monastery. They are to be shot on sight. I repeat, shot on sight.'

Bruce said, 'Looks like it's time for the turkey shoot. Get Max and Jane back here pronto.'

Up ahead, blocking the passage, were four goons disguised as monks. Bruce rolled a stun grenade down the passage. Lois and Jane shot them on their way through to the entrance of the old section of the monastery. The big old oak doors years ago would have been impenetrable and were a magnificent display of workmanship considering they had been built hundreds of years ago. Yet, especially between the doors where they came together with lock and chain, they were no match for Bruce's door breaching explosives, which allowed them to pass through easily to a set of stairs that went down into a dark, large, musty smelling room with three tunnels disappearing into the darkness.

'This place,' Jane said, 'has been hidden over the years, and may have been forbidden by some spiritual order, hiding long forgotten sinister acts, secrets created by twisted minds and unimaginable frightening truths that lie here in the darkness.'

They found some old cobweb and dust covered lanterns with the candles burnt only halfway down. They lit the lanterns, their meagre lights casting shadows over the walls of the tunnels, creating imaginary images of creatures. Max said being scared of the dark was just the result of an overactive imagination.

He said, 'There is nothing in the dark that's not there in the light.'

So, they headed off with their lanterns as companions. They went into a room on the left with a stone slab and drain hole at one end. Next to that was an old looking, open leather satchel containing all sorts of implements. A chill ran down their spine when they tried to imagine what went on in there. A cold silent breeze suddenly entered the room, and it felt like they had walked on someone's grave. There was a smaller room through an opening with steel rings concreted into the walls and chains hanging from them and a bundle of straitjackets on the floor. Strangely coloured moss was growing up through the cracks in the floor that gave off the smell of death. They wondered how anything could grow in such a cruel place away from fresh air and warm sunlight. There were cobwebs everywhere; they had to keep clearing them with the lantern. Over near a window that had no purpose at all was a large web with the most venomous looking, large, green and orange spider. The smaller web next to it had a nest of smaller spiders, the same shape and colour as the large one.

Jane said, 'There shouldn't be a cold breeze anywhere down here – there's nowhere for it to come from – but if you hold up the lanterns, look at that breeze. It's gently moving that big cobweb like something or someone was touching it.

'Jesus,' Lois said, 'can we get out of here?'

Max said, 'You know, I have just worked out what all this is, and why nobody has been down here. This, my friends, is where the monks, a long, long time ago, kept the lunatics who were given to them. There was nowhere else for them to go. This was their lunatic asylum.'

*

The three girls, Hope, Jemima and Naomi, were taken down to another section of the old asylum. This section had electric lighting and was currently being used to contain the girls who wouldn't give in and toe the line. They were being kept in the old asylum cells, and as this human traffic Syndicate system had been going on for years, there were fourteen of them in cells awaiting movement, or death if they didn't comply. Hope, Naomi, and Jemima were added to the cells. The other girls had been there for a long time and were anxious to hear what was going on in the outside world. Particularly when Jemima told them about the super-fit old dudes, they wanted to know more.

Naomi said, 'That's all we know.'

The fat monk, if that's who he was, sitting on a chair in the corner said, 'Shut up! Bloody women, can't stop talking, yap, yap, yap ...'

The youngest of them all, Hope, smiled and winked at them and put her finger to her lips.

She whispered, 'From what I have seen, we will be free and safe soon. I just know it.'

*

The Spiders had come to the end of the tunnel. They had no idea they were being followed by three men in the dark behind them. The door at the end of the tunnel had a sign on it that said, "Washroom. Do not enter while red light is on". There were two buttons on the wall; the green one said, "Fill" and the black one said, "Empty". They made the mistake of going in.

Inside the room, which was round, were steel rings and chains and concreted into the wall with a concrete seat that ran around the entire room. In the wall and ceiling were water nozzles and a large manhole drain with bars across it in the middle of the floor.

Lois said, 'How awful to be chained to the wall and washed like an animal!'

'We've seen enough,' said Joe, 'We've got dirt to scratch and eggs to hatch.'

The door was locked, and worse still, water started pouring out of every nozzle.

'Shit!' Bruce said. 'These podgy monks have a fetish about drowning people.'

The water was rising slowly. Max said they would have about an hour before they drowned: 'Someone, get over there and get that door breaching stuff on the bloody door!'

Jane volunteered. The plastic explosive was like putty that moulded to any shape on the door and in the cracks where the hinges were. The Spiders used the explosives with the blasting cap at the end of the fuse so they could detonate it with a match.

Joe said, 'It's starting to get beyond a joke in here. Put two of them on, and come way back here with us. You know the drill, Jane.'

With ears blocked, mouth shut, *boom, boom*! the steel door

was blown to pieces. The three men on the other side were different as they weren't dressed as monks – but they were all dead. The one with the teardrop mouth had a large fragment of steel sticking out of his head, and his eyes looked like they were poking out on sticks and his mate had the door handle and locking device hanging out of his stomach.

The Spiders found another tunnel entrance. This one was full of more cobwebs and critters scurrying along in the dark in front of them. As they got further up the tunnel, they could see a light coming into view. Carefully, they approached where the tunnel ended, and what they saw they would never forget. They couldn't be called cells, they were cages – full of young girls.

Lois took the opportunity to use her arrow gun. The dude in the chair now had the feathers of the arrow decorating the middle of his forehead. Bruce, Jane, and Lois took the girls to the basket winch. Joe and Max stayed behind to clean up. They knew their way around from the tour they'd had the day before. As they went down a dark tunnel they hadn't been in, they could hear someone calling out. They followed the sound to a dark room with their torches. It was hard to see Lydia bolted to a slab with steel straps over her legs, stomach, shoulders and head.

Joe said, 'Shit, Max, look up there.'

A thin steel rod with a sharp point and barbs was suspended above her head by a thin cord which had been set alight and was burning through. Joe got on Max's shoulders and grabbed it as it burnt through.

She said, 'I am known here as Lydia, but my real name is Wendy, and we were all stolen from London.'

*

The so-called abbot received the call that the gold was on its way to the basket for delivery, and the basket was to be sent to the bottom of the mountain. Bruce, Jane, and Lois could hear someone coming. They pushed the girls further into the bushes and watched. He lowered the basket, a buzzer sounded and he started bringing it up. Having now seen the routine, Jane shot him and dragged his body into the bushes. When the basket arrived, Bruce pushed the lever forward to stop the pulley turning and swung the basket onto the concrete landing.

'Come and look at this, ladies,' he said.

They looked in the basket – there were ten gold bars.

Lois said, 'Well, there are supposed to be a hundred of them. That's ten trips they must make.'

Jane said, 'We have enough people here to carry them one at a time into the bushes, so let's keep sending the basket down. I will lie in the long grass and keep watch with my rifle with the scope and laser beam.'

Wendy, who had been Lydia, said, 'We can't go yet. There are three more girls with me.'

'We already have them. Just keep up with us as we clear this place,' said Bruce.

*

Four goons were coming up the stairs to the oak door where Wendy, Max and Joe were. Joe lit a door breaching plastic explosive and threw it down the stairs. Goodbye to four goons. They still hadn't found the abbot, but it was more important to get the girls down to safety, so they headed out to the basket. On the way, Max rang Peter, who said he was on his way.

When they met the others, Max said to Jane and Lois, 'Put the girls into groups of four ready for the chopper, and as soon as the chopper arrives, load the girls immediately. We need a really fast turnaround each time.'

Another basket with ten more gold bars arrived and Bruce and Max lugged them into the bush with the others. They heard the chopper coming. Jane and Lois had the girls ready to go. Peter hovered just above the ground, the girls jumped in and they were on their way to freedom on the oval where they were almost pushed out, and back Peter went for the next load. Five trips were made. On the last trip, the chopper took fire from somewhere in the monastery so the pilot wasn't game to show himself above the drop. The basket was back at the top where Bruce, Jane and Max were the only ones left.

Max said, 'Quick, all in the basket.'

They jumped in, and he pulled the lever. The basket had the last of the gold bars, so it was a heavy load. About halfway down, two of the four cables on the basket tore away from the basket, and as they were both on the same side, it tipped sideways. They were hanging on for dear life. Although the boys were helping Jane to hold on, time was running out for how long they could last.

Then there was the fantastic sound of blades thrashing the air and the helicopter appeared next to them. With Joe holding the ladder in the open door, he threw it across to the basket and Jane climbed on and into the chopper. Next was Bruce, up the ladder and into the chopper. Max was straddling the side of the basket when bullets started pinging off the side of the rock wall. There was nowhere to hide, and the next two shots hit him in the side and the leg. He could barely hold on any longer.

Then the strangest thing happened. Jane jumped back into the basket with a light training parachute harness.

She said, 'We have come down to about the same distance from the ground.'

She roughly attached it and she pushed him out of the basket. Joe threw the ladder back for her and she was back in the chopper. She grabbed her rifle and Peter banked around in a big arc. There he was, the podgy abbot, leaning over the cliff edge firing at the basket. A red dot appeared on the abbot's face, and he was dead.

Max had earlier rung Harrigan and had given him the location of the gold. As usual, he, the police and medical support were waiting at the bottom of the mountain.

Max came floating down and almost landed in his arms.

Harrigan said, 'As bad as you are, Max, I would stick to flying.'

They loaded him into the ambulance and took him away. The Spiders' cars were still there, and off they went to the hospital to check on Auntie and support Max. They couldn't wait for Max and Auntie to be released from hospital, but even then, they would not be fit enough to go to Belgium.

Chapter Thirty-Four

The Syndicate had their own communications system within the dark web with coded messages. The alert would come up on their own normal phone message system to go to the dark web for the coded message.

Zilla read the message, crossed over to the dark web and read the coded message: "You are not dead yet because we need you at the moment. However, that could change in a minute if you fail. A black ops team called the Spiders is coming for you. They are old but very good at what they do. We are moving you with the girls to another country first thing tomorrow. A van will come for you at 9 am. Be ready to move." They would be using The Syndicate's private jet from Brussels Airport to Venezuela, a fourteen-hour trip to the Bolivar International Airport.

During the flight, one of the girls was making a cup of tea in the galley when she saw in the drawer a cigarette lighter matches and smokes. None of the girls smoked but she pinched the cigarette lighter and the box of matches next to it.

When they arrived in Venezuela, they now had a one-hour flight from Caracas to Angel Falls with a company called Conviasa. However, Venezuela has a high risk of kidnapping and human trafficking, crime and wrongful detentions. Zilla knew now why they were here: the girls would be worth a lot of money for The Syndicate, and there would be plenty of buyers waiting for the opportunity.

The four goons watched Zilla and the four girls transfer from the airport to Caracas and board a six-seater aircraft for the trip to Angel Falls. By the look of them, the girls would be worth a small fortune, the goons said, and that was why they booked their fare to Angel Falls. That day was Sunday and the company called Conviasa had two flights a day only on Sundays and Thursdays, but that suited the goons. They had certain supplies to get ready and people to notify. For Zilla and the girls' own safety, The Syndicate had booked them into the most out-of-the-way accommodation at Kavac, a remote indigenous village with warm yellow adobe huts inhabited by the Venezuelan people. Accommodation was hammocks or simple rooms with a bathroom and cold water, and a generator for a few hours at night. Surrounded by jungle, waterfalls and caves, it was certainly the middle of nowhere.

Chapter Thirty-Five

ASIO had been tracking Zilla but had been told not to intervene. They had tracked her as far as Venezuela but had lost her. Harrigan had received the names of the last four girls to be found. They were Sarah, Zoe, Amy and Molly.

Harrigan had a lengthy conversation with them about the dangers in Venezuela. He was really concerned and was thinking twice about letting them go. He knew he would be sending them into a den of thieves, cutthroats and kidnappers and a place that was poor and unhealthy. He hoped he wasn't sending them to their deaths. However, he knew deep down the Spiders were the best chance, the only chance, of getting the four girls back alive.

After the Spiders had resupplied their survival equipment before they left, Harrigan got the necessary permits and clearances for their weapons and their survival equipment to travel with them. He arranged for their weapons and survival gear to be delivered by military aircraft, dropped by a net basket parachute into Caracas at 4 pm on the day after they arrived.

Venezuela is a very rich country with very poor people.

The system they used was simple: if someone had something you didn't, you took it.

The Spiders flew with Turkish Airlines from Brussels to Venezuela, a fourteen-hour trip. When they arrived, they made enquiries using their official identification badges. Not that they needed them – you could get any information you wanted for a dollar. They were told four girls and a woman had boarded the plane to Angel Falls three days ago. When they booked their one-hour flight, they learnt there were two flights the next day and they only flew Sundays and Thursdays. The morning flight was booked out, but they could have four of the six seats on the afternoon flight. (The six seats on the morning flight had been taken up by the goons following Zilla and the girls.)

*

Once the girls and Zilla landed, a tour operator, paid a considerable amount by The Syndicate, would get them to Kavac privately. If they'd gone on the normal tour, it would have taken four days and three nights to get to Kavac, but they weren't there for a tour, so it would only take them two days and one night. Trekking through the jungle, they passed impressive waterfalls and rock formations, swam in the Canaima lagoon, walked through the water tunnel of the El Sapo falls and navigated the Churun and Carrao Rivers. And on the afternoon of the second day, they arrived at Kavac. The girls saw where they were staying.

Molly said, 'I can't sleep in a hammock. I keep falling out.'

Zilla said, 'You four will be in the huts, two in each hut, and I will sleep in a hammock. You can't go anywhere. It's jungle all around with predators like giant anteaters, giant armadillos, jaguars, pumas and vipers, green anacondas, giant otters, three-toed sloths and a variety of monkeys. If you stay in your huts at night and don't stray from the village through the day, you will be quite safe. I only plan to stay here for two days, where you will be traded to the highest bidders. I'll be going back; who knows where you will be going?'

The Spiders arrived in Canaima too late to do much. They stayed at the Compamento Ucaima Jungle Rudy Hotel. The next day would be hot and busy. They had been flying for a total of fifteen hours, and they were buggered.

The six goons who had arrived that morning, who knew where they were?

Chapter Thirty-Six

Sarah and Zoe were together in one hut, and Amy and Molly in the one next to it.

'We've got to somehow get out of here,' Amy said to Molly. 'I think this will be our last chance before we are, one by one, auctioned off to some filthy weasel just for his and other's pleasures.'

'Do you think you could remember your way back?'

'Some of the way, I think. I'm sure I'd get lost along the way. We need to talk to Sarah and Zoe. Let's all get together late tonight and see if we can come up with a plan.'

When the four of them were together that night, they agreed to try and talk to one of the villagers. They picked a girl, as they thought she might be more responsive. With sign language and broken English, play-acting and some sort of baby talk, the girl agreed to take them at first light.

The girls borrowed two machetes and followed her out of the village, shaking their heads and giving the silent action by putting their fingers up to their lips. Hopefully, she would get the message not to tell anyone where they were going. About five hours later, they came to a waterfall with a big pond at the bottom. The woman pointed and mimed the action of swimming. It was stinking hot, so in they went; the water was cold and refreshing. After some time, she called them out by waving her arms, and off they went. Along the way, she showed them things they could eat, rainforest fruits such as açai and cocoa. She stopped at a small shrub and pointed at what the girls knew was guava and they also passed a small grove of bananas. She pointed at a tarantula and play-acted that you could cook it to eat.

'No way!' they said to each other.

It was getting late when they reached another waterfall. Around the lake were coloured Amazonian flowers with the scent of sweet perfume. The village girl pointed to a small cave, a slit entrance almost concealed behind a curtain of water. They could just see it if they looked hard, but they had to swim in the lake to get to it. She pointed to the water at a striped catfish and mimed the action of eating, but when they looked around, she was gone.

The sun was going down and the curtain of water had a mystic tangent sparkle to it in the fading light.

'I think we should all get ourselves into that cave before it gets dark,' said Molly, who was fast becoming the leader. 'We can sort ourselves out in the morning with what we can do to make ourselves more comfortable. We will gather wood for a fire inside the cave entrance for warmth and security from predator animals getting into the cave. We can gather some of the foods that we have been shown and find out what that noise is further inside the cave. One thing is for sure – we are not going anywhere near that woman they call Zilla. I'd rather be eaten by a puma or eat ten raw tarantulas. Tomorrow's another day.'

They woke early the next morning due to an uncomfortable

sleepless night, but for the first time in a long time, they felt free.

'Maybe,' said Zoe, 'this is the first step to getting home.'

They cut some bamboo, peeled the string off the outside and lashed some of the poles together to make a small raft to float the food and firewood across to the cave. They also took some poles over to lash together as an internal door to block the entrance at night from would-be predators. The cave looked like a likely place where animals and critters would lurk and call this place their home.

As they went further into the cave, the bats were disturbed and flew beside them. Over their heads, the walls became wet and slippery and had a strange yellow glow, and the noise of running water was louder. The further they went the darker it got. They pushed their way through the dark and were getting worried they would have to spend another the night there. The noise was even louder, and the darkness had been left behind.

They couldn't believe what they saw – an internal waterfall with a pool of froth and bubble. The whole scene was telling them to come on in and stay a while. There was an opening up high where the water and light came in. This was obviously where they would stay, where the light and fresh water was. It was just a matter of getting past the section that was dark. There was no musty smell, as the water was bringing in the fresh air. So, now they had water and food and fresh air.

*

Zilla was beside herself. Once The Syndicate found out she had lost the girls, she would be dead, and those coming to bid for the girls would be really pissed off. The worst part was, she knew there wasn't much she could do about it. She certainly wasn't going into the jungle looking for them.

There must be something I can do, she thought. She didn't have the money to pay the villagers to find the girls. That would have to come from The Syndicate, but she would have to tell them what happened and that would mean a quicker death for her. No, that wasn't going to happen. She was going to have to bluff this out.

Chapter Thirty-Seven

The six goons following the girls were a day in front of the Spiders, pushing through the jungle toward Kavac to kidnap the girls, and they didn't care what they had to do to get them. All six of them were the scum of the earth.

The goons camped that night near a swampy area with a "Danger, quicksand" sign not far from their camp. The head goon, whom they called Shifty, got up to relieve himself and walked into the quicksand. The more he wriggled around to get out, the deeper he went. He was sucked down fast; the more he fought against it, the more of his life it took. The hard ground was only a couple of feet away, but he was just out of his reach of the tufts of undergrowth on the hard ground. He could feel the damp sand circling, crushing his legs and pulling him under.

The other five goons had been drinking heavily, so they were out like a light and didn't hear Shifty calling out. In the morning, they were calling out for him, but no response. When they saw the quicksand sign, they knew where Shifty had gone. The bloke now controlling the goons was Chico.

He said, 'We will be at the village this afternoon. The woman should be on her own, so it should be an easy steal.'

*

Zilla had managed over a period of an hour to get through to the head man at the village.

She said, 'You have some people working on the outskirts of the village. If they see someone coming, will they come and tell me? Is there somewhere you can hide me? Tell them the girls and I went two days ago.'

He smiled, showing just one or two yellow teeth, and nodded his approval.

*

The goons were getting close now, but they had already been seen by the villagers and Zilla had been warned of their arrival and taken to a hut that wasn't part of the village. Four of the five goons surrounded the village but didn't go in. Chico walked into the village and asked to see the woman with the girls. The chief told him they had gone two days ago, but he was welcome to stay the night if he wished.

'Do you know where they went?'

The chief said he thought they were going back to the big smoke. They had their own guide.

Chico said, 'We will stay here one, maybe two, nights and leave.'

He told the chief there were five of them, and he whistled them in. The chief wasn't a man of the world, but he could tell these men were no good and not to be trusted, and there was something about the woman that wasn't right as well. He was sure the girls wouldn't have gone off unless something was wrong. Their disappearance, the woman and the goons were all connected somehow. He would get six of his biggest men to be ready and watching for trouble day and night while they were here.

The next day, the Spiders arrived and were told the same thing.

'Two days ago, they all go back to big smoke. You can stay here if you like. Only cost small amount of money.'

They said they would stay till they sorted things out. They were shown to their huts; Lois and Jane in one and Bruce and Joe in the other. They were really buggered from carrying their packs on their backs with all their recovery and camping gear. They were told the generator would only run for two hours a night; after that, they only had their torches.

They decided to have a meeting while it was still daylight. The girls went to the boy's hut. Joe said he thought they had been given a load of bullshit.

'If the girls and Zilla had gone back to Canaima, we would have seen them along the track through the jungle. No one strays off the track because of the quicksand and predators, which is why the guides carry a rifle. Has anyone seen those other shifty looking blokes in the huts further down? What are they doing here? Remember what Harrigan said: kidnapping and human trade here are rife. I wouldn't be surprised if they followed the girls here from the airport to kidnap them. Anyway, something is definitely not right, and I think we should stay here until we get some answers. Like I just said, I don't like the look of those others, so keep your gun close to your hand day and night.'

Jane said, 'Well, I think, in the morning, we should sit down and quietly tell the chief exactly why we are here and show our credentials. It might just be enough for him to tell us what's really going on here.'

They all agreed.

The evening meal wasn't quite one star – a small piece of striped catfish, a piece of cassava root and leaves, a banana, açai and guava. Lois and Jane decided while they were here, they'd be eating their small cans of bully beef, of which each of them had six. Everyone ate together with the villagers in a thatched shelter called a house wind, with tables made by the locals. The five goons, as the Spiders called them, ate at a table by themselves and spoke to nobody, but everyone agreed they weren't here on holidays or to visit the Angel Waterfall; they were certainly up to no good. If they were after the girls and had been told what the Spiders had been told, they wouldn't have believed it either, which is probably why they were still here.

Lois said, 'I saw one of the villagers taking food to an isolated hut at the end of the village. You don't suppose ...?'

'No,' said Bruce, 'they wouldn't all fit in that small hut. But in a small village like this, it would be difficult to hide four teenage girls and a woman like Zilla.'

They rounded up the chief the next morning. It was a difficult conversation, but eventually, with some sign language and with the English he could understand, he smiled and they all shook hands.

He pointed to where the goons were staying and said, 'All bad, all bad.'

'Yes,' they said, 'all bad, very bad.'

So, now they thought he knew who they were, the good guys, they asked him for the story. He said the girls had run away from the woman. She knew these men would be coming and asked him to hide her when they saw them coming.

He said, 'She is in that hut down there by herself, but I don't know where the girls are.'

'Well,' Jane said, 'I don't think they could make it back to Canaima by themselves, and they won't have any survival skills. When night comes, which has happened twice since they've been gone, the predator animals and vipers could have already killed them and dragged them away, or they could have been swallowed by a green anaconda.

The chief said, 'There are many waterfalls and caves here in a big area.' He drew a small circle on the ground and said, 'Me here,' then drew a big circle and said, 'Big smoke.'

They said, 'Canaima?' and he nodded his head.

He drew another circle in between the others and placed five stones in the circle.

From all this, they said, 'Canaima is twenty kilometres away from the little circle. We already know that, so the circle in the middle is ten kilometres from here, and the stones in the circle are the caves and waterfalls, five of them in a ten-kilometre radius.'

'It is more logical that the girls would go for that,' Bruce said, 'but how would they know which way to go? They could be wandering around in the jungle forever.'

'I don't think so,' Jane said. 'I'm willing to bet the girls got some directions from one of the local village girls before they left. They wouldn't go out into the jungle knowing nothing. They have no sleeping gear and no tents, and no protection. Where would you and I go, Lois?'

'The caves and the waterfall.'

'That's right,' said Jane, 'and you'll find that's where these girls have gone. The question is, which one?'

That afternoon, they sat down to decide which one they would go to first.

Bruce said, 'Looks like there is one just a couple of kilometres from here.'

'No,' said Lois, 'it's too close to the danger they've just left. I think they would want to get as far away from here and Zilla as possible, and they would use all these caves and waterfalls along the way as stepping stones to get there.'

'Jesus,' said Joe, 'do you think they're smart enough to do that?'

'Well,' said Jane, 'they were well educated at the best schools available, so they must be smart. I know "smart" doesn't necessary mean they would have any survival skills, but between the four of them, hopefully they've worked it out. But all this depends on how much information they were given.'

'Right, so which way do we go?' said Joe.

They all said, 'The stepping stoneway, the opposite way to where the closest one is, and we leave in the morning.'

Chapter Thirty-Eight

The goons had been watching these newcomers closely and they knew the chief must have given them some sort of information that they didn't have, because they were packing their gear to leave in the morning. After the newcomers had gone, they visited the chief again, this time with more vengeance.

Zilla had been watching all the action from a window in her hut, and she had also watched the newcomers pack. She was certain they were the black ops group called the Spiders. Jesus, they were old, but she had already been told that, hadn't she? She decided, after they had gone, she would talk to the chief herself.

After the Spiders ate a can of bully beef and headed off, the goons headed for the chief's hut, all watched by Zilla. The chief was hesitant to give them anything, but they were threatening him with a gun, so he gave them just the direction to go in – and then they shot him. From the back of the hut came three of the tribesmen with their machetes. They buried a machete in Chico's head, just like they would with coconuts – then all three were all shot. The four goons, who'd started off as six, packed their gear and headed off, with Pedro now calling the shots.

Zilla's main aim was to get the girls back, so waiting in the village would amount to nothing. She quickly packed what she had, checked her gun and how much ammunition she had – fifty rounds, hopefully, would be enough – and took off after the goons. So, the Spiders were after the girls, the goons were after the newcomers and the girls, and Zilla wanted the girls back, but she would have to go through the Spiders, the goons and the treacherous perils of the Amazon jungle.

*

The girls were as settled in as comfortably as they could. They had two machetes which would give them some protection from predators. They had been venturing out further into the jungle each day, following animal trails that they thought might lead them to more water. They had woven thin bamboo strands together and tied them together onto four bamboo poles like a small trampoline. They could carry their wood and food with one of them on each corner, and they took that wherever they went.

Sarah said, 'Look, we have plenty of time on our hands while we are deciding where we go next, so we should gather enough materials to make a stretcher and thatched cover to sleep under. We have all the materials here to do that.'

Amy said, 'We could all work together to get them done one at a time.'

They added a bamboo door inside the entrance and made a fire pit from the rocks in the area, thankfully having stolen the lighter and the matches on the plane.

'There's nothing you can't do if you work as a team,' said Zoe.

*

The Spiders made good time and by morning they were at the first waterfall, although Bruce still thought they should have gone to the closest one first; if nothing else, they could have taken it off the list. When the Spiders reached the waterfall, they were so impressed with what Mother Nature had thrown up, they just sat on a large rock and let the scene swallow them. Looking up from their rock perch at the face of the high wall in front of them were at least six waterfalls down the left side of the cliff. Some were twin falls and others varying distances apart.

Joe said, 'These separate falls must be from a river that splits and divides into separate channels before roaring over the cliff top.'

The noise from the falls forced them to raise their voices to be heard. Shrubs and trees were clinging to the sides of the cliff, and looking up from their perch, they could see the familiar rainbow just above the mist and droplets in the air where the water cascaded over the edge. Down below where they were, the usual small birds, butterflies and dragonflies were cooling themselves in the fine spray where the water plummeted into an array of rock pools along the bottom of the cliff wall.

Now they would split up and start looking for the girls, checking for caves, particularly ones that could be hidden behind the curtain of the falls. Bruce and Jane walked down halfway and started looking, and Joe and Lois started from where they were now. They would meet up at the last waterfall and set up camp for the night. They were hoping there would be four more of them.

Bruce said to Jane, 'I wouldn't be surprised if those goons were not far behind us. They aren't going to stay in the village now that we're gone, and they are after the girls to sell on the human trade market.'

*

Pedro and his three goons were about three kilometres behind the Spiders. They would get themselves a little closer but not close enough to be seen. They had no intention of killing them till they found out where they were going, who they were and why they were there.

What the chief hadn't told them was that the villagers had animal traps dug with pits full of sharp, upright bamboo sticks covered over with soft brush. There were also sharp slingshot bamboo poles about a foot off the ground. All these were within the so-called ten-kilometre radius that everyone would be moving around in.

Zilla's plan was to casually follow behind, let them do the work and kill each other, if that's what happened, and when they found the girls, she would do some killing of her own.

Chapter Thirty-Nine

The Spiders had found nothing yet, but were experiencing more unbelievable sights. Even though they were buggered from the day's hike, the falls, even though they were noisy, with their cool and calming magic gave them back their energy. They set up camp in a cool place near the falls, and although they weren't cooking, they lit a fire against the cold and predators. They weren't expecting anyone, as it was too early in the hike and the Spiders thought the goons wouldn't do anything till they knew more about who the newcomers were and where they were going. The Spiders put out a picket with the rifle on two-hourly changeovers in case large predators like the puma and jaguars came into the camp at night. They only had small, thin one-man tents that were no protection against a large animal. And the picket could keep the fire going.

In the morning, they ate the contents of their third bully beef can along with some guava. They had a good supply of teabags and coffee and an endless supply of water. However, they hoped they would all be out of the Amazon rainforest before the last three cans of bully beef ran out. They resupplied their water and moved out in the direction of where they thought the next waterfall would be, and the tramp through the hot and humid jungle began again. By midday, they were exhausted from the heat and the weight of their packs. They took a break under a ceiba tree. This one was at least seventy metres tall with a massive trunk and distinctive buttress roots. Not far away was a tucuma palm with rings of thorns around its trunk.

Jane said, 'The local villagers use the fruit from this tree to make flour.'

Lois went off to find a place to relieve herself, even though she needn't have worried about someone coming along to see her. Then came a blood curdling scream.

'Where are you?' Joe said.

She had fallen in one of the pits with the sharp bamboo poles.

She called out in a distressed voice, 'I'm down here.'

'Jesus,' Joe said, 'you are the luckiest woman in the world, Lois.'

A large three-toed sloth had fallen in on the spikes and Lois was lying on top of it. They had to put a rope around her legs and shoulders to pull her out horizontally so she wouldn't get spiked by the sharp poles, that might have been poisoned.

It was really more like a thirty or forty kilometre area within the circle the chief had drawn, and it was all hard going. Pushing through the ever-changing lush, damp foliage and dense undergrowth, they had already crossed many lagoons and travelled through dark areas where the thick canopy blocked out the sun. They had sloshed through grasslands and swamps, through large areas of bamboo and tucuma palms. This was truly a hot, humid, damp and shitty place that they had to track through to see the wonders of nature's world and her amazing waterfalls.

'With an early start, we should make the last set of falls by midday tomorrow,' Bruce said.

They had one of their bully beef cans and went to bed. Lois was the last two-hour picket when the sun just made the top of the canopy. The birds had begun to sing, and they could hear the movement of the inhabitants of the jungle getting ready for the day's activities. The first of the morning dewdrops were plonking themselves on the tops of the one-man tents from the trumpet trees above them that were covered in damp moss, with green stringy creeping vines wrapped around the trunk and hanging from their branches. The wet, thick undergrowth was all around them, hiding mysteries of the world.

Jane said, 'One in every ten of the world's plants and animals is found here in this rainforest – and we will soon be trudging through it again!'

They packed their gear and headed off.

Both Zilla and the goons were only a kilometre behind them and each was beginning to think they were wasting their time. It was starting to look like these newcomers were professional bushwalkers out to visit all the falls, as they had done nothing to suggest anything else. They kept plugging their way behind them, as they were virtually heading in the same direction as Canaima. Pedro had tangled with the thorns on a tucuma palm and his leg looked like it was now infected, and he was slowing the others down. Zilla was also the worse for wear, as she had twisted her leg in a porcupine's hole and was walking with the aid of a piece of bamboo pole, but she was in sight of the goons.

*

Back in the village at Kavac, the young girl who helped the four girls escape was now worried that she had left them out there with no jungle survival skills, and since the threat of the woman and the others had gone, she decided to ask them to come back to the village for their safety and her piece of mind. She found them carrying their makeshift carry rack with food and wood and was amazed at their survival skills. They agreed to go back but left everything they had made in the cave in case they had to hurry back there. Their clothes were tattered and smelt, even though they had washed them several times in the lake, their hair was matted and looked like birds' nests, so even if they only had a clean-up in the village, it sounded good.

The young village girl, whose name was Tamaroa, told the girls what had happened after they had left. Her understanding of English wasn't the best, but with perseverance they could have a conversation. She told the girls she thought the two women and two men were the good ones, and they might have even been looking for them, as they left after talking to the chief. The other five were very bad.

'They are the ones who killed my people,' she said, 'and one of the bad men was killed, so the four others left to go after the good people and the woman followed them all.'

'We can't just stay here,' said Zoe, 'Maybe we can catch up with the men and women we think are looking for us.'

'We wouldn't get five kilometres from here before we were lost,' said Amy.

Tamaroa said she could take them as far as the big round waterfall but no further.

'There are kidnappers looking for young girls to sell if we go any closer to Canaima,' she said.

They washed properly and did what they could with their hair. There was no need to take food as Tamaroa would gather it along the way, and they had each taken a container to get water from the falls.

Tamaroa said, 'We will catch up to them in a day and a half. I know all the short cuts and easy-going tracks.'

'When we get closer, we will run into the bad people first. We will need to go around them at a distance,' said Sarah.

They were young and fit and knew where they were going, so it would be a fast trip with only a one-night stopover, and Tamaroa knew exactly where that would be. The girls were excited. There was finally some light at the end of the tunnel.

Chapter Forty

The Spiders heard it long before they saw it. They were still a kilometre away and even if they had been stone deaf, they would have heard the roar of millions of tons of water thundering over the cliff. When they arrived, none of them was ready for what they saw. They stood there and stared in disbelief.

There were just no words for the scene in front of them – a deep, almost full circle canyon with waterfalls all the way around, some dropping two and three levels before the last long drop. The amount of water gushing down the rock wall was mammoth, the noise was deafening and the thick curtain of water, particularly as it reached the bottom of the drop, was something to see. All the way along the rocky wall, wherever there was water nearby, were green bushes clinging to the sides of the rocky cliff, and an array of Amazonian flowers – yellow and purple bromeliads, orange and yellow lobster claw flowers, red and green monkey bush vines and patches of lovely yellow orchids among the falls, they were the creative finishing touch of an artist who was, of course, Mother Nature.

The force of the water was powerful and it covered the whole canyon base with a fine mist. They were using their high-powered binoculars to search for caves behind the curtains of water. There was only one cave in the whole canyon.

'Bingo, there it is!' said Jane.

No one heard her, so she had to physically poke them. It was useless to try and talk above the noise where they were, so they moved around the base of the canyon.

'Looks like we are all getting wet,' said Lois. 'We are all hot and sweaty, so it will be cooling and soothing. The last one in has the first picket tonight,' she said, and in they went.

Passing under the curtain of water was an experience, like being massaged by ten giants' hands as it pounded over their heads and cascaded down over their shoulders. It felt like they could sit there and meditate for hours. The cave walls were wet and slimy with light and dark green mosses, and while they were still in some light near the entrance, they could see ancient stick-figure sketches of fish and animals on the walls.

'Someone else was here a long, long time ago,' said Joe.

The spindle shaped roots of the trees growing above them hung down through the roof of the cave, and who knew how much rock was above their head. Their voices echoed along and down through the cave, and their torches made eerie shadowy figures along the walls and caught blind cave spiders as they searched for their prey. They turned off their torches and were suddenly in a world of darkness and stillness. Out of nowhere, a cold breeze whispered past them from somewhere in the cave. The four girls they were looking for weren't there.

Lois and Jane said, 'I think we have seen enough, and we are all wet and cold. We need to get out into the sun again.'

After being pounded by the curtain again, they found a camp site away from the wind if it came, and a large rock overhang if it rained. They gathered firewood for the night, set up their tents and discussed their plans for tomorrow.

Joe had the first watch and was relaxing by the fire with the rifle, that he had just cleaned and fitted the lens of the night scope to, across his knees.

He turned to pick up his cup and said, 'Shit! What was that?'

He was sure he had seen someone move. There were no trees or bushes to blur the vision, it was a clear night and the man in the moon was awake.

Jesus, he said to himself, *I'm sure I saw a small something. Must have been an animal.*

But he would be on his guard. He told Jane, who had the midnight till two o'clock picket, about the strange event earlier on, but whatever it was, it wasn't seen again. Lois relieved Jane at 2 am and they were sitting round the fire talking, when they both saw it – a small head with a huge amount of black fuzzy hair behind a smooth rock about a hundred metres away, which then disappeared. The boys came out and looked, but who or what it was had gone.

Next morning, they had packed up and were about to leave when they saw a very small native man with a mass of black hair.

'This was who we saw last night,' said Lois.

He was beckoning them to follow him into the jungle. They followed him, and he kept turning around to see if they were still there. They were getting deeper into the Amazon rainforest, surrounded once again by dense undergrowth and tall trees as straight as an arrow. They were being taken away from their goal of finding the four girls when they suddenly came across the remains of an ancient city.

'Some of these cities here in the rainforest have lain hidden for thousands of years,' Jane said, 'and were home to populations of more than 10,000 people, more than 2000 years ago. They were teaming with settlements in pre-Hispanic days, and they weren't just thatched huts. Some of those lost cities were complex structures with well thought-out waterways and reserve systems.'

The little man was now calling them in to the ruins. This lost city was no longer a thriving beehive of activity, nor was it majestic in appearance, but was now just a crumbling ruin overgrown with vines and bushes from hundreds of years of growth. But when they looked more closely, they could see evidence of long-ago man-made structures, their features unrecognisable due to the distance of time.

They followed him in through the rubble to where work had been done to restore a small part of the building. It looked like there were fifty or sixty of these little people living quietly hidden away. Lois saw a long piece of white rock that said "City of Gwarf". These little people were called gwarfs, not dwarfs. They were shown to an area where a small gwarf girl was lying on a thatched bed. She might have been three, and she had the measles, something that they obviously had never seen. The Spiders opened their advanced medical kit, which the gwarfs gathered around to look at. They gave them tablets to keep her temperature down and showed them how to read the thermometer.

They couldn't stop smiling and saying, *'Blew der, blew der,'* which probably meant 'thank you', and patting them on their heads. Yet there were little men waiting outside with spears and machetes which worried them, but they were all smiles when they left. It was late now so they decided to go back to the canyon falls again for the night and strike off again in the morning.

*

The goons had arrived at the canyon falls just in time to see the newcomers appear from the jungle.

Pedro said, 'They have been here a day already. Why are they coming from that direction now?'

Zilla had caught up and was at the circular falls, watching the goons who looked like they had mixed with a dozen gorillas. They would be easy to knock over now, but she would wait. Maybe they would all do it for her. But where were the girls? She would still have to be patient.

Pedro decided it was time to find out who these people were. He fired a shot at them from behind a rock, and the noise echoed right around the canyon.

'Let's see what they do now,' he said.

The answer came quickly. A bullet ricocheted off the rock and sent slithers of rock up, cutting his ear.

'Well, that's our answer,' he said. 'They're no ordinary bushwalkers, are they?'

The girls and Tamaroa had heard the shots and had a bird's eye view of who was where. The good people were down in the canyon and the scum were up behind a large rock. As the girls began to move around the top of the canyon towards where the Spiders were down below, two pumas came out of the jungle and crept along behind them. They were on a dry section of the canyon where a large part of the wall had broken away, leaving a gap too wide to cross. Now they were trapped between the pumas and a long way down to where a waterfall plunged into a large rock pool, the waterfall with the cave.

Molly said, 'I can't believe we have come this far, and now we are going to die!'

The Spiders had been scanning the top of the canyon watching for the goons when they saw the four girls.

'Look up there,' said Joe, 'It's the girls.'

'Yes,' said Bruce, 'but look what's coming up behind them.'

Lois and Jane looked through their binoculars and could see the two pumas stalking the girls. Joe fired some shots at them, but they were too cunning; they got down low and continued to crawl along towards the girls.

The problem was every time the Spiders stood up to show the girls they were there, the goons shot at them.

Joe said, 'I'll fire at them to keep their heads down, and you lot move across where the girls can see you but the goons can't.'

They were now standing on the edge of the rock pool directly beneath where the girls were, waving their arms and trying to get the girls to jump. But the girls were obviously scared.

Jane said, 'Well, in a minute they won't have a choice, will they? The pumas are so close they must be able to smell their breath.'

The girls were shaking with fright. They realised the cliff was the only way out, and they knew it wasn't guaranteed that jumping was going to be all cookies either. The pumas were getting ready to pounce, so over the edge they went. When they appeared on the surface of the water, so did the bullets.

'Why would they be shooting at someone they want to sell?' said Lois.

'Because they're mental morons,' said Bruce.

They screamed at the girls, 'The cave behind the waterfall – go, go!'

The four of them swam towards the waterfall and disappeared behind the curtain of water.

Then they saw an amazing event – one of the pumas launched itself over the cliff into mid-air. What a fantastic picture it would have made! The puma wasn't falling helplessly out of control but seemed to be gliding like a bat. It hit the water like a sea eagle diving for fish. The puma surfaced, swam to the edge and slunk off into the jungle, while the puma's partner watched the whole thing from the top of the canyon and backtracked through the jungle.

'How could one shoot such a majestic animal in full flight like that?' they said.

'You would never see something as heart-stopping as that in five lifetimes,' Jane said.

They all agreed that Mother Nature would thank them for the decision – well, someone would one day. It just seemed cruel and unfair to kill them, even though they were going to eat the girls if they could.

Now everything was out in the open, the puzzle had come together, and everyone knew where they stood. Pedro had moved away from the protection of the large rock to get a better look at what was happening in the bottom of the canyon. He made a wide berth through the jungle for protection from the shooting. His ear was bleeding consistently, with nothing to quell the bleeding, and he was unaware of the blood trail he was leaving behind him. He found a concealed spot where he could see and fire at will. The gentle breeze carried the puma's bad breath smell from behind him and invaded his nose, and he felt the hot breath on his neck, just before the puma tore a hole in it and dragged him away.

The goons were concerned why Pedro had not returned. Shakey went looking and found blood on the leaves and undergrowth and drag marks into the jungle.

Jesus, he said to himself, *half of us are dead, all because of these girls. We should just kill them instead of selling them. It hasn't been worth the trouble.*

*

The goons and Zilla had seen the girls jump and swim to the curtain of water, so they were either hiding behind the screen of water or there was a cave behind there. However, they weren't the only ones who had been watching all the action.

Inside the cave, it was pitch black, and the girls had nothing to light it up with, so they sat near the entrance where they still had some light. Down somewhere in the darkness of the cave, they thought they saw a flickering light that looked like fireflies round a fire at night. It seemed to be there one minute and then gone. As it got closer, they could see it was the flickering from several small flames, and they were moving toward them.

Molly said, 'What do we do now? Do we jump back into the water and get shot or do we stay here and get eaten by the fiery monster that's coming?'

'No,' said Zoe, 'we stay here and see what it is, and then if we must, we get back in the water.'

'But what if this thing can swim?' said Sarah.'

'Then we are fucked,' said Molly.

As the flames got closer, they could see torches being held by strange little people with fuzzy black hair. They were wearing skimpy loincloths and the women wore nothing to cover their breasts. (Zoe thought that was an excellent choice as she hated wearing a bra.) Each man carried a long spear and a machete, and each woman a long thin knife in a thatched sheath.

'Well,' said Amy, 'we are now going to get cooked in a pot by these little cannibals.'

'Don't say it,' said Zoe.

'What?' said Sarah.

'Out of the frying pan into the fire.'

When the gwarfs arrived, they were all smiles.

'That's a good start,' said Molly.

Zoe said, 'It depends on what they're smiling about. Anyway, you will probably be first one in the pot. You've got more meat on than us.'

'Spoken like a trustworthy friend,' Molly said.

The little people, whoever they were, couldn't speak English, but with one or two universal words and actions, they showed they wanted the girls to go with them.

'What do you think?' said Amy.

'It's the best offer we've had today,' said Sarah.

It was a long cave, but walking next to the flame torches gave them a warm feeling and a sense of security. In the distance, something was moving around near the roof of the cave. When they got there, it was the scariest sight the girls would ever see in their lifetimes. Dozens of ten-metre large anacondas were hanging down from the roof of the cave, slithering and sliding in and out of large holes, all of them with their large mouths open and hissing loudly to block the way through.

'I hate snakes!' Amy said, 'They make my skin crawl. Last year we did a study of these green anacondas. They are not venomous, but they are the heaviest and the largest snake in the world, they can grow to ten metres long and weigh over two hundred kilos. They crush their prey with the powerful muscles in their body and can gape their mouth bigger than their body to swallow a human.'

The little people used their torches to move them out of the way till they were past them. One of the anacondas swung down close to Amy's face and was staring at her. She was frozen on the spot with fright. One of the gwarf men came back and dragged her away. She was trembling and sobbing and scared stiff of what might still be up ahead.

When they got to the end of the cave, they could see a little better. A tunnel had been made that looked like it went a long way.

*

Zilla had run out of patience. What she wanted was in the cave. She worked her way around to the edge of the curtain of water and jumped in. She entered the cave and switched on her torch; it was so dark her torch only gave her enough light to see a couple of feet in front of her. Too late, she saw the snakes hanging from the roof. The largest one detached its jaw, put its mouth completely over Zilla's head and began to swallow her, its body expanding to an unimaginable size as Zilla slowly went down into the snake's body. In fifteen minutes, there was no sign off Zilla.

*

The Spiders were considering their next move. The girls had been in the cave by themselves for a long time, but if the Spiders went in now, they could be trapped when the goons came in behind them.

'Look up there,' said Lois, 'There's that little man again. He's trying to get us to follow him.'

'We have more important business here than measles,' said Jane, so they ignored him, and he left.

They needed to get these goons off their backs before they entered the cave to get the girls.

'The little man is back again,' said Jane, 'and he has four tribal women with him. Look at that. What's he doing that for?'

He patted them on the head one after the other, then waved.

Does anyone of us dumb bastards know what he is doing? He is trying to tell us something ... That's it!' said Joe. 'He has four women, and he is telling us "four girls". The little people have them.'

'Bullshit!' said Bruce. 'They're in that cave. How could they possibly have them? I think one of you girls should go with them and see for yourself. And make sure you don't come back alone.'

Jane said she would go.

'Good,' said Bruce, 'We will be here when you get back. Let's see if we can make these three goons look like two.'

*

Out of the goons who were left, one said, 'Its bloody obvious we are out of our league, and we should have realised it days ago. We should just sit back now till we all get back to our environment.'

The rest of them agreed. They would just watch and follow till they got back to civilisation where they had a better chance of getting the upper hand.

Chapter Forty-One

Jane returned and told them the girls were safe at the lost city ruins with the gwarfs, and that there was a tunnel from the cave to their village that they had dug over many years. The girls didn't want to come back and show themselves to the goons, so the little man had come back with four of the village women. The Spiders knew they would be followed to the hidden city ruins, but they would deal with that when the time came. They were all safe for the time being, as the little warriors had encircled the ruins with their spears and machetes.

The little women of the village were ecstatic about Sarah and Amy's blonde hair, following them around, touching their hair and giggling. The Spiders thought the chief's name was Tonga, as he kept pointing to himself, saying, 'Tonga, Tonga'. With a lot of picture drawing in the dirt, they realised they were going to be escorted to the edge of the jungle at Canaima, and then the little people would go back. The little warriors said someone was following them; the Spiders smiled and gave them the thumbs-up sign. They knew the goons would not be doing anything there; they would wait for the opportunity back in Canaima.

They stayed one night in Canaima, at the Waku Lodge where the girls had their own room where they showered and started to look good again, and they were able to be guarded easily with the Spiders' picket system. There, they were able to buy something better to wear than what they had. Their clothes had tackled the Amazon rainforest and come off second best, meaning they hardly had any clothes on at all. The Spiders took it in turns in a chair with the rifle outside the girls' rooms. The goons must have been too knackered to make a play for the girls that night.

The Spiders booked their return to Caracas in Venezuela on a six-seater aircraft. There were now eight of them, so they got Joe and Lois with Sarah and Zoe on the morning flight and Bruce and Jane with Amy and Molly on the afternoon flight.

Next morning, Joe and Lois got ready for the first flight back to Caracas. The girls had been given strict instructions not to be more than six inches away from Joe or Lois until they could get a pair of handcuffs. Then they would be handcuffed, Sarah to Joe and Zoe to Lois, so they couldn't be dragged away in the crowd. As soon as they landed in Caracas, Joe and Lois rang Harrigan to send some support as soon as possible, and they would have a signal for their watchphones when the support landed.

*

Back at the small aircraft terminal in Canaima, Bruce and Jane with Molly and Amy had been waiting till the afternoon Canaima plane was ready to load for Caracas, when two goons arrived and said, 'Get out of the way. This is our flight.'

'Not for about three months from now,' said Bruce, and shot

one of them in both kneecaps. Then he said to his mate, 'Well, what about you? Is this your flight?'

'No, sir!' he said, as he carried his goon friend away.

This aircraft was a sister to the one that had left that morning, the same sort of six-seater aircraft, but with a different tail number. The surprise was there was a copilot, which meant only four passengers could go.

'That's strange,' said Bruce, 'It means the company has lost one paying passenger.'

There was no one else booked to fly, as it turned out, so the four of them were good to go. They asked why there were two pilots. The copilot said the one flying the plane was being assessed to join the company. They couldn't argue with that. The plane left the earth behind, and they heard the wheels go up with a thud.

*

That morning, Dominic Rodriguez was getting ready for work. He was the scheduled pilot that day for the return trip to Caracas and Canaima. He had showered, and his uniform was hanging on the towel rail in the bathroom ready to wear.

'Who's that?' he said and went to the door.

The three goons from the jungle were still persevering.

'Hello, are you Dominic Rodriguez?'

'Yes,' he said.

They shot him in the face and took his uniform. One of the goons' friends was a shonky pilot whose name was Miguel Lopez. The small airline used many contract pilots, so a different pilot today was not unusual. Miguel had on the company uniform (he was about the same size as Dominic so his uniform fitted) and his ratings for VFR and IFR were in order. He was given the flight plan details, weather and clearances for the tower. His goon friend was waiting for him in the plane. They loaded four passengers and took off for Canaima, where they would pick up another four passengers, these ones worth a lot of money.

*

Harrigan wasn't there when Joe rang on Tuesday. Joe had just begun to talk to Harrigan's second-in-charge when he saw what was about to happen. He only had time to say, 'Venezuela. Need urgent help. Police arrest', when a police van with sirens blaring almost ran them over. The side door opened, and they were all pushed in.

Venezuela was rife with false arrests and imprisonments. They were taken straight to an out-of-session court hearing. It wasn't a good outcome. Joe and Lois were charged with kidnapping and sentenced to death by a lethal injection. The two girls were charged with prostitution but were told there could be a way out for them if they cooperated with certain people in high places. Prostitution also carried a death sentence, so what were the girls going to do?

Joe and Lois were put in the same cell due to overcrowding.

'Half the people in here,' said Lois, 'wouldn't be guilty of anything due to the corrupt government and police force filling their pockets with contraband and money through the black market. Some of them may never be seen again. How the hell are we going to get out of here without help?'

'I wouldn't know,' said Joe, 'but it had better be by Friday or we are dead.'

*

They had been in the air for about forty-five minutes when Jane she said she didn't recognise any of the scenery down on the ground.

Bruce said, 'That's because we are flying south-east instead of north-west.'

'Are you sure?'

'Yep, I don't think the sun has changed to setting in the east.'

There was another strange thing they missed; they weren't given headsets this time, and the goon and the pilot were both wearing parachutes.

Jane said, 'Look, I didn't say anything earlier because I wasn't sure, as we never got a good close-up look at the goons in the jungle, but I'm almost positive now the one posing as the copilot was one of them.'

'Show me our map,' Bruce said.

They both agreed that with the fuel range this plane had, they were on their way to Guyana, and they had only about an hour to do something about it.

'Well, we can halve the threat,' she said, and shot the goon in the back of the head. The pilot panicked and said he was just getting paid by the goons to fly the plane. He was only doing what he was being paid for. He didn't know anything else.

'Which was bullshit, of course,' said Jane.

Then he opened the door and jumped out. The controls were currently on autopilot, so there was no immediate panic.

Jane said, 'I don't suppose there's anyone here that can fly this thing, is there?'

'Flying isn't the problem. It's landing it that's the hard part,' said Bruce.

Amy and Molly had been asleep until they had heard Jane's gunshot and seen the pilot jump out. Molly said her dad had a plane like this. She had often flown with him in the copilot's seat and had been taught a little bit. She knew where everything was in the cockpit, but she had never landed a plane, but she had watched her dad do it many times. They took the parachute off the goon and pushed him out.

Bruce said, 'Does anyone want to put this on and leave while they can?'

Everyone said, 'No!'

Bruce put Molly in the cockpit with him and said, 'It looks like it's only 200 km back to Caracas. How's the fuel?'

Molly said, 'Plenty,' and began to show him where everything was in the cockpit: the speed angle, the altitude flaps, the wheels down lever and the rudder pedals that controlled the yaw (swerve and twist) of the direction of the plane turning left or right. She took him through simple procedures like "too slow, nose down", "too fast, nose up", the speed in landing pattern on approaching 80 km, "power off, flare up" on landing.

'Keep flying the plane through landing to taxiing on the runway, and good luck,' she said.

Chapter Forty-Two

The small aircraft with the Spiders and the girls was about to take its turn in the queue to start the landing approach. They had advised the tower that it was a mayday situation, and the tower was helping with the landing.

'Alpha Tango Zero six, you're too high. Come down to three hundred metres ... yes, that's good. Wheels down now. Watch your speed: 80 km/hr. Come a little left now for line up ... Looking good, half a metre to touch down. Flare up now, nose down slowly for front wheel contact ... Congratulations! Nice landing, sir.'

Molly leaned over and gave him a kiss, and when they got out, so did the others. They decided to ring Joe and Lois to bring them up to date.

Lois had hidden her watch phone in her undies. She felt her phone vibrating down in her pants. She went to the corner of the cell while Joe watched in case a guard came.

'You're where?' said Jane, 'Shit! Keep your phone on buzz and we will message you, so you don't have to talk. Send me the airport locker number where our survival gear is. Hang in there. We are coming.'

Jane and Bruce hired a V8 Land Cruiser, picked up the rest

of the survival gear that they hadn't taken into the jungle and rented a villa on the outskirts of town. They buzzed Lois for what she knew about the layout where they were being held. She said it appeared to be a smaller cell area off the main jail; inside was a central steel walkway with five cells each side. The cell they were in was the first one from the door, which was steel and double bolted, so they didn't think the door breaching explosives they had would damage the door.

Jane and Bruce took a drive to Vista Hermosa jail the next day to make a plan. Joe, Lois and the girls were in a small annex on the outskirts of the main prison. The stone walls were old and petrified with age, and that's where their door breaching explosives would be used. The gates into the area were simple high wire gates that would cause no problem for the Land Cruiser. The next day was Thursday, so no time to waste. Jane sent the message: "Tomorrow, 5 am, stand by". They got a message back telling them the guards' room was opposite their cell, and the girls were in the next cell to theirs. "Block your ears, mouth shut and face away" was the message back.

They went back to the villa and explained it all to the girls.

'We will smash through the gate, reverse the Cruiser flat out into the old stone wall, Amy will jump out and hook the grappling iron in the hole and we will make a bigger hole. In goes the door breaching explosive, and *boom*. Molly will be ready to dive through the hole and throw the stun grenade into the guard's room,' Bruce said. 'I'll be out of the car by then and will kill the guards, get the cell keys and let everyone out. All out through the hole, Jane behind the wheel and we are gone.'

Next morning, they came flying through the closed gate.

'Shit!' said Bruce. 'What are they doing out here at 5 am?'

The guards were in the yard kicking a soccer ball.

'Change of plan.'

Jane drove the cruiser straight into them and Bruce opened fire. The whole thing lasted thirty seconds, and the guards were dead. The side steel door was wide open. They rushed in and threw a grenade into the guard house, where there was now only one guard. Jane grabbed a bunch of keys and unlocked all the cells and they were gone in less than ten minutes.

*

The Carnival festivities were in full swing, with thousands of people dancing in the streets. Everyone had some sort of face mask, and all the women wore bright colourful clothes. They ditched the car, bought themselves a face mask each and two throwaway phones and joined the crowd. An hour or so later, they joined the locals and visitors having coffee at the restaurants on outside tables, but they were careful not to sit together, Bruce sitting with one group and Joe with the other.

'We won't get caught again,' Joe said, 'Anyone comes near us this time, police or not, they're dead. Don't wait for a discussion; just pull the trigger. The whole town's full of scum. You could see why Venezuela is known as the bottom of the earth.'

There were two men in suits sitting nearby giving the Spiders too much attention. Eventually one came over, showed his badge and said, 'What you did this morning will hardly be an issue.' Joe put his gun away. 'With what's going on here at the moment, there are much bigger issues here than you lot. Harrigan's message for you is, "We can't get in here at the moment with military air support as it's too hot politically. Come home by civilian air if you can." But I don't think you can get out. They have all your details and photos. You might have to go into hiding, bide your time and wait for the military when they can get here to get you.'

'That's no good,' said Joe, 'We won't last the distance. We will all be dead or disappeared by the time they get off their arse. We've worked with these dummies many times. By the time they fiddle with themselves and have another doughnut and coffee, we'll all be in a hole in the ground somewhere. But thanks for the heads-up about our photos and our details being known.'

They returned to the villa to regroup and stay out of everyone's way. The next day, Bruce and Joe went to separate car rentals and hired two 4×4 Ford Ranger twin cab utes. They spoke to several shonky locals who said they could get them out, but they looked like they couldn't be trusted. They got the name of a man called Mario Fernandez, who flew gold from the illegal gold mines in Venezuela to Brazil. They returned to the villa with the vehicles and rang Mario.

So, this was now the plan. Drive to Gran Sabana, 520 km away, stay one night. Drive to a hidden air strip in the jungle, board an old Douglas DC3 full of gold from the illegal Venezuelan goldmines and fly to a place called Pacaraima on the north edge of Brazil. Mario would charge 500 dollars for each person. Take a plane from Cumbica Airport in Brazil to Australia, twenty hours flying. They packed their gear that night and left at first light.

Brazil was much the same as Venezuela with violent crime, including mugging, armed robberies and carjacking, particularly during Carnival time. They wouldn't be going into the city, so they should be okay.

'The trip won't be without problems, I guarantee you that,' said Lois. 'The whole trip will be long and dangerous, so don't kid yourself.'

The track was rough and sixty to eighty kilometres was the best they could do.

'There is nothing along the 520 kilometres according to the map, just a meandering gravel road that really is just a dirt track most of the way, probably a ten-hour trip,' said Bruce, who was in the rear vehicle with Jane, Amy and Molly.

Up ahead was a brightly coloured half-jeep, half-truck full of what looked like poorly dressed locals, and they were bogged in deep sand. The Spiders had been warned about stopping in isolated areas. They decided to risk it this time as they was eight of them, with drawn weapons. Jane and Lois stood on the roof of their vehicle with a rifle and handgun aimed at the crowd, while the boys hooked up a tow rope and pulled them out. They drove off, watching the kids with runny noses jumping in and out of the truck. They could see a small siding off to the left and a Suzuki Jimny half hidden behind some bushes, but they were right onto it, as they were communicating with each other on the throwaway phones. Joe's voice came over the phone.

'Do we have any actual hand grenades left?'

'You bet,' said Bruce.

'I'll leave it to you then, mate,' said Joe.

Jane stopped the Ranger just past the Suzuki. Bruce got out and looked inside it. Yep, they were goons, all right.

'Hello, boys. Do you know what this is?'

He showed them the grenade in one hand and the pin in the other hand.

'Have a nice death,' he said and popped it in through the

window. It hit the deck. *Boom*! The brightly coloured jeep truck pulled up, and within minutes anything that hadn't been damaged by the grenade had been removed from the Suzuki. The Spiders watched it all, and with grins on their faces headed off again.

It was almost dark when they arrived in Gran Sabana, and luckily, they found suitable accommodation because Zoe and Sarah had the symptoms of malaria. Luckily, where they were staying had a supply of quinine, and hopefully they would have enough time to visit the clinic tomorrow.

There was a knock on the door, and a man, who said he was a friend of Mario's, said he had come to collect the 4000 dollars for the flight to Brazil. He said he would be back tomorrow to take them to the hidden runway.

'Not going to happen,' said Jane, with everyone in agreement. 'When we are on the plane, he gets his money, not you.'

'Well,' he said, trying to spook them, 'no money now, no plane ride.'

'That's okay,' they said, 'then there's no need for you to be still standing at the door. Piss off!'

'Well,' Lois said, 'we're either in the shit for a plane trip, or we have just prevented a scam. Time will tell, won't it?'

The next morning, they left Bruce behind in case the scammer came back and headed for the clinic. Bruce was cleaning the rifle and packing the survival gear into boxes when two men appeared. He made sure they saw him slam a full magazine into the weapon and cock it.

'How can I help you?'

They both threw their arms in the air. The taller one said his name was Mario Fernandez, the pilot and owner of the plane, and he would expect the money as soon as they got on the plane.

Your money is guaranteed,' Bruce said. 'Did you send someone here yesterday to collect the money?'

'No, I did not,' he said. 'This is Dominic. He will come back for you at last light, when the plane has been loaded. We fly only at night to avoid detection. You can take a ride with the vehicles into Brazil when we land.'

The Spiders arrived back with a supply of malaria tablets.

'Bloody bastards,' said Joe, 'trying to scam our money ... but it sounds like we are good to go.'

Chapter Forty-Three

Although there was a lot of water to flow under the bridge yet, the Spiders felt they were winning. But they were getting anxious.

They left the vehicles at the accommodation and were taken by an old blitz truck to a secret location in the jungle where there was a long, cleared landing strip. As they got close, they could see lights filtering through the tall jungle canopy, which stretched upwards like long native spears, and they could hear the low murmur of voices. Flame torch lights disappeared into the darkness that lit up both sides of the runway. At one end of the runway was a large, cleared circle where an old but magnificent DC3 Dakota sat ready to go. At the other end was a low full moon bathing its gentle light onto the runway, caressing the forest as they came together as one, like a mother cares for and feeds her child. The whole scene was quite eerie, but at the same time, had a romantic touch. Beyond the flickering lights was a different jungle, full of mystery and fear, and as nightfall approached, the sounds of the jungle began to fall away. Uncertainty hung in the warm, wet air as the creatures prepared for the long night ahead, while others began their night hunt for food.

While they waited on the edge off the clearing, Lois and Jane said, 'The plane looks very old. Do you think it will be all right? It doesn't look safe.'

Joe said, 'Girls, what you're looking at is a Douglas DC3 Dakota twin engine monoplane first flown in 1935. It can carry nearly three tonnes of cargo or twenty-eight passengers. It has a cruising speed of 300 kilometres per hour and has been flying for almost a century. It *is* old, but it's super safe. Inside, you won't find anything that resembles luxury.'

There were six guards with rifles circled around the plane to protect the illegal gold that they had just finished loading, along with boxes of contraband. The sounds of silence were broken by gunfire from the dark jungle and three of the guards went down. Mario had the port engine running and was firing up the starboard side, which coughed, spluttered and belched blue smoke; then it fired and both props were up and running.

Mario stuck his head out the high cockpit window, calling out, 'For Christ's sake, get in!'

As the plane started moving down the runway with bullets peppering the fuselage, the Spiders and the four girls ran alongside and one by one scrambled through the door. Materialising out of the night sky was a Black Hawk police helicopter, with a voice through a speaker screaming, 'Stand down!' But they were already wheels up and flying over the rainforest, heading southeast over the regions of Venezuela's Bolivar State and the Guyana highlands to and the northern border of Brazil and Pacaraima.

Bruce fancied himself as a bit of a pilot by now, so he went through to the cockpit and sat in the copilot's seat to talk to Mario.

'Did you have a full tank when we started?' Bruce said.

'Of course we did,' and treated the questions as an insult.

'Well, don't get excited. You'll see why I asked when you look at the gauges.'

'Jesus! We must have taken a round in the port side tank when we took off. We won't make it to Pacaraima; we will be about 300 kilometres short. We will bypass Pacaraima and fly directly into Brazil along the Caroni River. We must have been flying on the smell of an oily rag, but we've had it now.'

Bruce went back to tell the others and glared at Lois for putting the jinks on them at the start, who said this trip wouldn't be without its problems.

'So, what you're really telling us is we are going to crash,' said Jane. 'Well, hopefully we can skim along the water like a duck.'

'Yes,' he said, 'we are going to crash.'

He winked at the four young girls and smiled. They looked back at him like a boxer dog with large droopy jowls and big sad eyes.

'There's the Caroni River down there now,' Mario said. 'It's a massive river, more than 900 kilometres long, from the Sabana to the sea. I'll keep us high as long as I can. These things have a glide pattern somewhere between an eagle and a rock. Hopefully, we can come down like a gliding eagle and not like a rock, so we can get as far along the river as we can. When we hit the water, if we are still the right way up, I'll try and get us close to the bank so one of the villagers will see us come down and help. If we can get close to the bank where it's shallow, we will bottom out and all will be good. Tell the others they need to leave the aircraft as soon as they can, in case they get trapped and we sink. We will talk again when we are all wet.'

They glided along just above the water for half a kilometre as close to the bank as they could. It didn't take long to stop once they hit the water. It's amazing how some things happen – when the plane hit the water, it skewed around, and when they had completely stopped, the port wing was on the bank, which was a couple of feet higher than the water. The wing now formed a bridge to the bank that they could walk back and forth to unload their gear.

There must have been a village close by. Kids, dogs, men and women started arriving to gawk at the plane and point and smile at them. Those who could speak a distinguishable English said they would help them carry their things to the village, and they were welcome to stay till they got sorted out.

Mario was going nowhere. He would stay with the plane and the illegal cargo. Mario was beside himself. How was he going to protect the gold and the contraband? It wasn't his; he was just delivering it, and the head goon, whoever that was, would not be happy if it all went missing.

Lois said, 'What's wrong with this place? Unless you're standing next to a tower, there's no bloody phone reception.'

They all sat down that night to get a plan for moving on.

Jane said she had been talking to the head honcho, who told her they were three days by dugout canoe away from the big smoke in Brazil.

'We will have to pay because fuel for the big V8 motors mounted on a frame on the back of the canoes is expensive. I told him we would need three canoes, and we would pay whatever it cost. We need to get to Brazil as soon as we can.'

Bruce said, 'You're not just a pretty face, are you? When do we leave?'

The head honcho said it would take him two days to

organise the canoes and guides to go with them, and the supply of food and fuel from villages further along the river. The Spiders and the girls spent the next two days doing what they called "make and mend", getting things ready for the river trip. They would keep the same split as before: Joe and Lois with Zoe and Sarah, Bruce and Jane with Molly and Amy. The third canoe would carry their gear. As soon as the head honcho returned, they were ready to go.

Chapter Forty-Four

The canoe drivers spent a considerable amount of time with a sort of safety brief. The seating arrangements were the most important. These rough looking canoes were very skinny and very fast, so to keep the balance required a left-right-left-right pattern of passengers. At full speed, there was definitely no movement that would cause a disaster.

Jane and Lois said it was like sitting on a skinny piece of bark going 100 kilometres an hour. When they got used to it, it was quite exhilarating, until Joe fell out. By the time they turned around and got back to get him, he had surfaced with a ten-metre long green anaconda wrapped around his neck and stomach. He had his fingers between the snake's body and his neck, trying to release some of the pressure. But the anaconda was too strong, and Joe was turning blue. The snake had dropped its jaw ready to swallow Joe headfirst. He was going under when the dude steering the canoe jumped out and made a metre-long slit with his knife down from the snake's head. The snake convulsed and vomited up Joe's head, covered in green and yellow slimy, thick liquid. Lois and the girls hauled him into the canoe and washed him down with buckets of river water. He was still alive but would take time to come back to some sort of normality.

They spun around and headed off again.

Lois said, 'Look at that … Did anyone see that? There it is again – look!'

The native steering the canoe said, 'That's a freshwater pink river dolphin. As they get older, they start turning pink, so they are known as pink river dolphins.'

He slowed the canoe down and said, 'If you look over there near that sandbar – you can see its head above the water – that's an Arrau side neck turtle. It draws its head in to its shell sideways, and they can grow up to a metre long.'

They reached the second village late in the afternoon. Joe was looking considerably better.

Lois said, 'I bet he never falls out of a boat again.'

The villagers heard what had happened to Joe with the anaconda, so that night the village elder invited them to sit around the fire so he could tell them about the mythical anaconda. The elder said all the villagers along the river and the rainforest had their own mythical stories of the green anaconda, the biggest snake in the world. The closer the villages in the eastern Amazon rainforest were to Brazil the more their stories told of the ancestral anaconda called the Grandfather, who guarded the door to the river, and chose who might enter and who might not. With the exception of the jaguar, the green anaconda held the most cultural significance with all the villages that lived in the rainforest. Some villages believed the river took the shape that the snake demanded. Other villages along the river believed the river took its shape from the snake's body with its curves, twists and turns, and that the ancestral green anaconda was part of the creation of the universe. The myths of the anaconda were many and went on and on, depending on who one talked to, and from which village. The anaconda spent most of its time in the water but was also found on the land in thick vegetation and often in trees.

'Jesus,' Lois said, 'I won't be able to sleep tonight. Look where we are all sleeping, with thick vegetation close by and look at all the trees. And after watching Joe's head come out of the snake, with all that green and yellow goo all over his head and face, I'll probably never be able to sleep again anywhere.'

When the elder had finished talking, they all quietly decided to hang on a little harder tomorrow. Zoe and Sarah weren't well, with another bout of malaria, so they all stayed another night where they were till the girls' temperatures came down, but they would need to see a doctor as soon as they reached Brazil. They had been taking chloroquine tablets, but if the malaria became severe enough, the girls might need intravenous artesunate to hone in on the infected red blood cell from the bite of the female Anopheles mosquito. This would be up to the doctors in Brazil.

They were getting close now to Brazil, just one more village only sixty kilometres away. But something wasn't right. A small boy had come down the river to warn them about the danger at the village. Villages close to Brazil had visiting teachers who taught the kids English, so they understood everything the kid said.

'Bad men come village, kill people. Many people run away. Bad men want gold. We say, no have. They say, where is gold? They shoot my father and four other people. They see you coming and hide in bush. I run to tell you they are waiting with guns.'

The boy then spoke to the canoe men in their language. They pushed the canoes up to the bank and got the gear they needed. Joe said, 'We don't need eleven people wandering around the jungle, and we can't leave the girls here by themselves.'

They left Jane and Lois with the high-powered rifle, both their handguns and a grenade, to mind the girls and the small boy. The men headed off with the three natives trailing behind.

Bruce said, 'They will be expecting us to be coming upriver, so let's go round the back of the village and come in through the jungle. That way, we should have the upper hand. The boy didn't say how many there were, but there's going to be more than two.'

Joe said, 'It's either the goons who have heard about the plane and the gold somewhere upriver and they've come to steal it, or the goons who were supposed to take delivery of it if we hadn't crashed. Either way, they're prepared to kill for it.'

They came in from the jungle, skirting the edge along the tree line. They could see the bodies lying in the centre between the thatched huts. They were about to enter the village when gunshots came from one of the huts and splintered bark from a tree next to a native's head.

'Whoever the idiot is in there doesn't realise a bit of straw and bamboo won't protect him,' said Joe.

One of the canoe men slipped around the back of the hut, cut a hole in it and quietly slit the gunman's throat.

'I wouldn't mind betting someone is watching the river,' said Bruce.

There were two of then standing on the bank smoking. Bruce and Joe came up behind them.

Joe said, 'How's the fishing going, fellows? Are they biting? No? Well, you won't be missing anything will you?'

They shot them both and left them on the edge of the water for the green anacondas to swallow. Suddenly, a single shot was fired and Bruce went down. He had been hit in the back and couldn't move his legs. Joe and a native saw where the shot had come from. They moved in close under the protection of the jungle and threw in a grenade. The goon was blasted up into the trees, parts of his body hanging from the branches like slabs of meat. The village people started filtering back in.

Lois checked her throwaway phone to find they now had reception. They rang the local police and ambulance, although Brazil wasn't that much better than Venezuela where corruption was concerned. When they arrived at the village, the police and ambulance said they weren't doing anything until they were paid.

Joe said, 'We have had enough of your corruptive shit', shot both police and pushed their car into the river with them in it. 'Get this man into that ambulance, or you're next.'

In a flash, they were all in the ambulance and headed for the largest hospital in Brazil, the Hospital das Clínicas da Fauldade de Medicina da Universiade de São Paulo and Bruce was taken straight into theatre. The Spiders booked two twin rooms for the girls, one for Lois and Joe, and one for Jane. They hoped Bruce would be going straight to the plane from hospital; otherwise, they would book him a room later if needed.

The Spiders took the girls to the hospital to outpatients to see a doctor and waited for another doctor for news on Bruce, hopefully not paralysed.

'Hello, I'm Dr Nicole Fenton. I have some good news. Bruce is a very lucky boy. The bullet missed the spinal cord, kidneys and pancreas. There is some ligament and tendon damage. He can't be moved for several days, but after that he should be fine. The girls are good to go, and we have resupplied their tablets. When they get back to Australia, they need to see their own doctors.'

Jane made some phone calls to the airport for scheduled flights home. What a surprise! Harrigan had booked eight first class flights to Sydney, open for whenever they needed them.

Chapter Forty-Five

The Syndicate was angry with what should have been a normal, simple operation. People were going to die, and they didn't care how many, but they would get the gold back. Although The Syndicate was just a gang of cutthroats thieves and murderers with a worldwide profile, they were very professional within their own system. So, they sent two new agents back to Hambleden for the treasure they didn't have yet, determined to get their hands on it. This time, they would send a higher class of killers, those who were not quite as expendable as the usual ones they dealt with; the others were cheap, and you know what they say about that – "if you pay peanuts, you get monkeys". This time it would be different. They had underestimated these Spiders for the last time.

The man known just as Budd had been issued an ultimatum by The Syndicate to find the gold and contraband or prepare his will. Budd was the head dude when it came to moving illegal gold and contraband for The Syndicate. He knew about the transport of the human cargo; as long as it didn't interfere with his cargo, it was acceptable.

Because the Spiders had flown illegally, they had not used their passports, which meant The Syndicate couldn't track them until Bruce's details and passport were used at the hospital. The Syndicate, through their dark web connections and officials in high places, obtained the whereabouts of Bruce and passed it on to Budd and his goons.

The Spiders visited Bruce in hospital on day three. He would be discharged the next day, and they would activate the tickets that Harrigan had organised. Three men in white coats arrived and asked the Spiders to leave while they examined him. They moved into the passage where they could still see him.

'They don't look like doctors to me,' Jane said. 'They wouldn't have the intelligence between them to put on a bandaid.'

They decided to go back in and saw two of them holding Bruce down while the other one was pulling the tubes out and about to give him an injection, calling out, 'Where is the gold? Where is the plane?'

They rushed in, shot the one with the syringe and knocked out the other two. They lifted Bruce onto a gurney, put on the goons' white coats and wheeled him out the side door marked Triage. Outside was an empty ambulance. Outpatients was close by, so Lois grabbed the girls and they were thrown in the back with the rest of them. Bruce was in the back with Jane, and Joe did the driving with Lois up front. They swung back to the motel, picked up their personal and survival gear, and headed off.

They had hardly got going when Lois said, 'I hate to have to tell you this, but we are being pursued by an old model Mercedes and one of those crazy coloured jeep things.'

They had seen these jeeps in Manila and Singapore. They were called jeepneys.

Joe said, 'This may be better than it looks for us. We need

different transport from this ambulance. The trick is to get rid of them but not destroy the two vehicles, which we can use. These jeeps have a large ute type tray with long seats down each side and a hard top roof open on each side. It would be perfect to take the stretcher out of the ambulance and put it in the jeep with the girls, and if we didn't get the Mercedes, it won't matter.'

The roads in Brazil were in fair condition, so they were able to pick up a fair speed on the outskirts of town. Those in the back of the ambulance decided to put the flashing lights on and Joe pulled over to the side of the road and waved the cars on, which was highly unusual. Joe then moved the ambulance over to right side, so they had to pass on Lois's side. As the car drew level, the passenger in the Mercedes looked over and smiled at Lois. He had a weasel face and possum's eyes.

She said, 'Hello there,' and shot him in the eye socket. 'Thanks for coming.'

The driver of the Mercedes pulled back behind the ambulance. The back doors of the ambulance opened, and a grenade came out and hit the windshield of the Mercedes and blew it to pieces. The driver of the painted jeepney was a bit more cautious and trailed along behind for a while. They waited till both sides of the ground were clear of trees and obstacles. The back doors of the ambulance were still open, so Jane pushed the magazine into the rifle and watched the little red dot bounce around on the windscreen in front of the driver. There was nothing each side of the road to damage the jeep, so she pulled the trigger. The jeepney bounced across the open space, coming to rest against the only tree for miles around. Bruce on his stretcher was transferred to the jeepney and the dead goons' bodies were put in the ambulance and driven into the swamp.

It was all aboard the jeepney, that looked like something from the circus. They made their clothes look like they were local villagers as best they could, and headed for Puerto Iguazu, 1500 kilometres away in Argentina, where Cataratas of Iguazu International Airport was. A twelve-hour flight would get them to Miami. They stopped at the next petrol station owned by Petrobras, one of the major petroleum companies in Brazil . They filled up and bought six twenty-litre fuel cans for the trip.

Joe said, 'If we ever get back, the government will owe us a lot of money.'

Jane said, 'Don't worry, I have it all documented.'

Lois said, 'I'll tell you what I think. If we ever get back, we keep away from Max and Jane's at Fairview. Every time we go there, we end up in the shit, like we are now.'

Two hundred kilometres along the way, Bruce, who was now actually sitting up, called out, 'Stop, stop! We've got phone reception.'

They all tried their throwaway phones, and bingo! Jane rang Harrigan and spent some time filling him in on some of the details.

'We are going to need a clearance and a lot of help at the borders of Argentina and Brazil in Iguazu. They may have our photos and details from the jail break, and you will need to change the plane tickets. We will be there tomorrow night for a flight out of this shit hole the next morning, if there's one available. We may not have a phone signal now till we get to Iguazu. I'll give you our throwaway numbers.'

Bruce was up now, walking around and sitting with the others on the bench seats that ran along each side of the truck. The stretcher was flung out the back. Up ahead they could see some buildings and people activity. The general store sold warm soft drinks, warm beer, canned food, women's long mumu dresses, men's shorts, shirts and a variety of miscellaneous items. The Spiders and the girls bought some clothes to look more like locals in the truck. Jane and Lois along with the four girls bought a mumu. There was also a petrol station and a small outdoor market selling local fruit and vegetables and handmade jewellery. A small village school class was under way under a thatched roof called a house wind, with a dozen or so kids, and alongside the house wind was a smaller bunch of kids and a sign that said "Kindergarten". Jane and Lois agreed it would be more of a child-minding place if anything, but they all had the mandatory runny noses.

As they were climbing back into the jeep, two beat-up looking Toyota Land Cruisers came flying out of the bush. The roofs had been roughly cut off, leaving raw sharp metal struts exposed. Someone in the first one threw a bomb into the general store and sped off. From the second vehicle, a satchel bomb was thrown onto the rooftop of the store, bounced off, landed under the house wind and exploded.

Lois and Jane said they would never forget the screams uttered by the children when the explosives went off, crying out in fright or pain from their injuries. The ones who weren't dead all had traumatic amputations. What senseless murderous action to harmless little children! This place truly was the bottom of the world, full of the scum of the earth.

Both vehicles tore off in the same direction the Spiders needed to go. They bought more fuel and prepared themselves for the action they knew would be coming.

Joe said, 'Well, if you want peace, you prepare for war.'

They knocked out the windscreen of the jeep. Lois was in the front with the rifle and a grenade, Bruce and Jane had their handguns, Bruce had Lois's powerful bow and arrow rifle and four arrows, and they had a grenade each.

There were four of these bastards, two in each vehicle. The bets were they would be waiting up the track to pounce.

Chapter Forty-Six

Bruce said, 'Show me the map. Where we are at the moment?'

They all looked at the map over Bruce's shoulder. 'See that?' he said, 'There's another track that parallels this one for twenty kilometres before it joins it. If we use this other track, we can conceal ourselves where the tracks join. And *we* will do the ambush, not them. They will get sick of waiting and will eventually pass where we will be waiting. Remember, we are the ones with the plane ride to catch, not them. The only ride they're going to get is in a coffin. And while you're killing them, think about what they did to those little kids.'

The second track was small but smooth, enough room for one car only. They made good time, travelling between eighty and ninety kilometres per hour. Where the two tracks met, they found a perfect ambush position, well hidden and facing where those barbaric animals would be coming from. When they arrived, it would be important to stop the first vehicle on the track. The track was narrow, so the second vehicle would be trapped behind with nowhere to go. The plan was to roll a grenade under the front of the first vehicle. They were beginning to think the killers might have gone back looking for them when they heard engines coming. They weren't far away. The four girls were told to lie down flat and stay there.

The first vehicle came into view. Lois made the little red dot dance on the windscreen in front of the driver and pulled the trigger. The vehicle she was in slowed to get a grenade near to the front and the underneath of the vehicle. The grenade lifted the front off the ground and bent and twisted the front-end structure. The second vehicle had nowhere to go, but they had some rapid fire weaponry that was pelting the jeepney. Bruce and Joe got out, using the jeepney as a shield. Everyone else did the same, as the firepower was too strong and rapid to stay in the truck. Joe took off through the jungle and snuck up behind the home-made convertible. He pulled the pin and lobbed the grenade into the vehicle. An instant kill, it blew the driver into the trees. The dude with the firepower was sent into the air and came down, impaling himself on a sharp structure that at one time held the roof up. Bruce had seen where the passenger from the first vehicle had gone, and he could see him now with his back to a tree for protection. Bruce loaded the arrow gun and fired. The arrow went through his head and pinned it to the tree.

'That will teach you for trying to get ahead of us. Good riddance to a mongrel,' said Bruce under his breath.

'We will be in Iguazu tonight, and this will all have been a bad dream – or a nightmare. Your choice,' said Jane.

Chapter Forty-Seven

Lois and Jane checked in with Aerolineas Argentinas and they were on the flight 7.15 pm that night to Miami, arriving at 6.05 am the next day, then a 1 pm flight with American Airlines to Los Angeles, arriving at 4.08 pm, all first class.

They parked the jeepney outside the airport and left behind what was remained of their survival gear, which wasn't much after their last encounter. As they walked across the tarmac to the aircraft, they turned to have a last look at the flea-ridden place they were leaving behind. Looking out a window in the terminal were –they couldn't believe it! – the three goons who were still after the girls. As they went up the stairs to the plane, Bruce gave them the finger. Joe had a bit more flare than Bruce. He pulled his pants down, bent over and showed them his bum.

The girls were old enough to drink alcohol but were reminded that although the drinks were free, it was a twelve-hour flight. However, they were all buggered and slept for eight of them.

'We will be landing in an hour,' the pilot said.

They ordered a bottle of white wine and Jane made a toast.

She said, 'We should be proud of ourselves for what we have all just been through and achieved. We have done it again with no loss of life, and with the luck that seems to follow us around. I'm sure we have all missed Auntie, and particularly Max, who says he is not in charge. But we all listen when he has something to say. And if he were here now, he would say, "Never let your successes go to your head, and your failures go to your heart".'

They all said, 'Hear, hear.'

The plane was on time landing at Miami International Airport. They had no luggage to be transferred (and lost), so they were shown to the first class lounge, where they could all shower and have a decent meal. They had a seven-hour gap before the flight to Los Angeles. The mumu dresses the girls were wearing were fairly daggy, so Lois and Jane went shopping with the girls for clothes for themselves and suitable clothes for the girls to meet their parents in Los Angeles. On the way, Jane, being the go-between, rang Harrigan and gave him an update. She said they would be wheels down in Los Angeles at 4.08 pm.

He said, 'Tell Zoe, Sarah, Amy and Molly their parents will be waiting for them. And, Jane, Max and Sue are fine, and we will include them in any celebrations that will obviously happen. The parents are ecstatic and are ready to give you Spiders anything you ask for in return for their children's safe return.'

He then told Jane the flight arrangements to Melbourne.

As they were about to board the plane in Miami, Joe got them all in a group and said, 'It's been a hard road to travel. You girls only know the half of it, but you will have some exciting stories to tell your children and grandchildren. We won't be coming with you when you meet your parents. That will be a very private family occurrence. We will be leaving you when we get off the plane, and I would think this would be our last long-distance travel. We are now, I think, long past being Tarzan and the Phantom all in one. And as I said, you will be busy with your parents when we land, so let's say goodbye here.'

The girls started to cry, along with Lois and Jane, and if one looked closely, the boys had a tear in their eyes as well.

The plane taxied to aerobridge number three. They told the girls to go down the walkway first. They waited till last, then the Spiders disappeared into the crowd.

'What time did Harrigan say our flight to Melbourne was? asked Lois.

Jane said, 'We're on United Airlines Flight 112, gate number 6, boarding at 5.30 pm. Wheels down in Melbourne, Tullamarine Airport at 8.45 am tomorrow morning. We've got an hour to amuse ourselves.'

Fifteen hours was a long time to be in a plane. On board, by the time they'd had a few drinks, watched a movie and swapped seats for a talk with each other, only five hours had gone by. Thankfully Harrigan had booked first class again and they were in a cocoon where the seat turned into a bed. A soft blanket, slippers and a shower bag were in the side compartment. So that's what they did – they slept. They awoke to an announcement they thought they would never hear again.

'Ladies and gentlemen, this is the captain speaking. We have begun our descent into Melbourne. The time is 8.05 am Eastern Standard Time. The weather is a warm sunny morning, 18 degrees Celsius. We hope you have had an enjoyable flight and hope to see you again when next you choose to fly United Airlines.'

The Spiders started clapping and the other passengers joined in. They heard the wheels go down and hit the runway. The air hostess made the last announcement: 'Ladies and gentlemen, welcome to Melbourne.'

Lieutenant Commander Harrigan was waiting for them.

'I just don't know what to say to you people, but I want this trip to be your last. If anything happened to any one of you and you didn't make it, my heart would be broken beyond repair. Arrangements have been made for your travel home. There are cars and drivers waiting with your name on a board. Jane will be going home with Rex Air from Essendon Airport, and a car and driver is waiting.'

He said he would be in touch soon, because the parents of the girls were arranging some sort of a welcome home to which they would all be invited. The Spiders all went back to their respective houses. The bad news was that when Sue had got home earlier, the goldfish were dead. Max was at the Bairnsdale Airport when Jane flew in with Rex Air. Both Max and Sue had completely recovered, and so had Maria. Nitro had sent a message saying, "Welcome home, good to see you all safe and sound."

Max and Jane's friends were interested in how their holiday in England went: 'It must have been very relaxing for you all.'

Max smiled at Jane and said, 'Yes, and an unusual way to spend a holiday, looking for hidden pirate treasure.'

All the normal maintenance needed to be done after a holiday. Weeks turned into months, and in a few weeks, it would be time for the quarterly trip to Max and Jane's at Fairview. The parents of the kidnapped girls had conducted a FaceTime session to decide where the welcome home party would be, given that the girls were from all over the world. It certainly wasn't going to be at any of the places the girls had been taken to. In the end, it was decided that they would hold the party in Australia. Given that each family had a mum and dad and two girls meant ninety-six people plus the Spiders and whoever was invited from Australia. The invitation said there were definitely no political people to be invited from Australia.

'Well, that's a pleasant surprise,' Max said. 'There will be no politicians there blowing their bags about the girl's safe outcome and twisting the facts around to get some political mileage out of it for their own selfish benefit.'

Chapter Forty-Eight

The party was to be the weekend after the Spiders' get-together at Fairview, and that's where they were now. The invitation was for eight Spiders: Max, Jane, Bruce, Sue, Joe, Lois, Bob and Maria, to be held at the Cruise Bar at Sydney Harbour, commencing at 5.30 pm. The dress code was cocktail.

The first thing the lady Spiders said was, 'We've got nothing to wear!'

Jane and Lois said, 'We're going back to Melbourne with Bruce and Sue to go shopping for suitable cocktail wear.'

Max said, 'Take Bruce with you and don't let him buy elastic top pants with his shirt tucked in. Someone explain to him what cocktail dress for men is; otherwise, he won't be allowed in.'

*

They were all at the Hilton Hotel Sydney getting dressed for the cocktail dinner. Bruce had outdone himself with a dark blue, open necked shirt, powder blue sports jacket and chino style, sandy coloured slacks, and he had chosen a dark blue and light blue pocket square. Sue was wearing a chic long skirt and crop combo, matching flat heel shoes and clutch bag. Max, who considered himself the know-all of the dress codes, wore a crisp white shirt, sports jacket with neutral pants, no socks and boat shoes; he had gone for no tie and a bright red pocket square. Jane had decided on a black two-piece jumpsuit, with a silver lace-up print off one shoulder, one long sleeve, silver trailing waist scarf, silver beaded clutch bag and silver heels. Not to be outdone, Lois was wearing a blue sleeveless, wide legged jumpsuit with a cross neck and pearl décor, white sandals and white clutch bag. Maria chose a floral print, watermelon red, elegant asymmetrical sleeveless twist dress with matching watermelon sandals and small white purse. Bob looked the part in a green sports jacket, light green striped shirt with a buttercup yellow pocket square and green suede slip-on shoes. Joe was the last to appear from the bedroom.

Lois said, 'Well, hello there, my lover boy, my hero!'

He was wearing a white sports coat and a pink carnation, a pink pocket square, sandy coloured flared pants, tan shoes and pink shoelaces, a polka dot vest and a pink tie with a big Panama and a purple hat band.

When they arrived, twenty-four girls rushed to them, yelling and laughing, some with tears in their eyes.

'See the effect I have on young women?' Bruce said, and with that came a flick on the ear from Sue.

'They all look upon you as their grandfather, you idiot.'

'Then, of course, there's me,' said Max.

'You're another idiot,' said Jane. 'Now behave yourselves, the both of you.'

The girls took their turns introducing the Spiders to their

parents, with hugging and kissing and shaking of hands twenty-four times.

The Cruise Bar was a fabulous venue, almost on top of the water in the Rocks area at Sydney Harbour. The band was playing soft seniors style music, obviously chosen by the parents and not the girls. All these girls' parents were very wealthy, so these girls would never know what it would be like to go without. They would always have the best that life could give them.

Max said, 'I hope they realise how lucky they are, and can give someone less lucky a helping hand, at least once in their life.'

Then came the embarrassing part of the night.

'Hello, ladies and gentlemen. My name is Lieutenant Commander Harrigan. It's been a wonderful night and very rewarding to see all these lovely girls here safe and well– and we all know who to thank for that.'

The whole room erupted in applause. Harrigan went on.

'I have known these wonderful and brave people who call themselves the Spiders for many years. They have survived many dangerous missions, all done in their senior years. The oldest of them is Max at eighty-two, the youngest is Lois and Max's wife, Jane who is seventy-two. When I think of what they have done in the past and recently, it's beyond belief. They won't be asked to put their lives on the line in the future, even if they volunteer – and I know they will. They will not be asked anymore for help. They have earned their time now in the long paddock. There is nothing they can't do. Max still thinks he can fly helicopters. When he flies, he makes it up as he goes along. There's nothing the others can't do either, from explosives to crack shots with most weapons. We want you to retire now while you're still healthy enough to still enjoy life, or your luck runs out and we lose you. Everyone in this room loves and thanks you from the bottom off their hearts. Please raise your glasses to the Spiders, one and all.'

Later that evening, Harrigan came over and said, 'Each one of these families will be sending you $1000 for your bravery in saving their children.'

'There's no need for that,' said Sue.'

'Don't be so quick to give away my money,' said Lois, 'that's $24,000 each.'

Max said, 'I'll only accept the money if we keep the rule: "everyone in, or everyone out". In other words, we keep $22,000 and give Nitro and Maria $12,000. They are part of the team. It's not their fault they weren't with us.'

Everyone agreed that's what should happen.

Max said, 'If everyone gives me their money, we could buy our own helicop--'

'--No bloody way! Our days of scary flying with soiled underwear with you, mate, are over!'

Chapter Forty-Nine

The Spiders had to return to the cottage in Hambleden to get the rest of their belongings and to say thanks and goodbye to the locals who had befriended them while they were there, particularly Anne, the direct descendent of Anne Bonny. They didn't mind going back. There would be no danger this time and the government had agreed to pay the cost, due to getting the girls directly home from Venezuela on the most direct route with no stopovers.

They flew back to London, collected their Land Cruiser at the airport car hire desk and headed off on the ninety-minute trip to Hambleden, arriving in time for lunch. The government had been paying the rent on the cottage as agreed, so they decided to go there and change before lunch.

Someone had been in the cottage while they had been away. The telltale cotton they used across the doorways had been broken, yet nothing had been disturbed or stolen. They rang Police Sergeant John Weir, who agreed to have lunch with them at the pub and discussed the break-in.

When the Spiders arrived at the pub, there were quite a lot of locals having lunch there as well. When they saw the Spiders, they all stood up and clapped, followed by lots of shaking of hands, kisses and 'Thank you for helping our humble town'. A loud whistle rang out.

Lois said, 'Yep, I know what that is. It's the lunchtime whistle. Everyone downs tools for lunch.'

Over lunch, Johno agreed there was nothing to be gained in an investigation when nothing had been stolen or damaged, but it was a concern that someone had been in the cottage.

*

The woman known as the Black Cat flew into Gatwick Airport from Rome and was to link up with the second contract killer at the London cable car, twenty-five miles from the airport. They would both be wearing a red scarf, and they were both scheduled to fly in on the same day, as near to midday as possible. The Butcher of Boston flew in from the United States into Heathrow Airport. He was an in-demand killer who was not known to fail. His M.O. was to dissect his victims' faces. The standard of his education was that he could spell "London". They met at the cable cars and took the ten-minute ride to discuss why they were there and how they would work together to find and obtain the treasure for The Syndicate. They were being paid a considerable amount of money, so The Syndicate would not tolerate a second failure.

*

The Spiders returned to the cottage after lunch to find a note pushed under the door that said, "Need to see you urgently, Dee, Town Hall". So back to town they went. Dee was at her usual spot at the front desk.

She said, 'I don't know ... I hope I'm just imagining all this because of what's been happening here, but there are a man and a woman looking at journals from the fourteenth to the seventeenth centuries. They have been asking me questions and what I know about Calico Jack and the rumours of treasure. They came right out and said they were here looking for the treasure.'

'Well, there's no harm in that,' said Sue, 'The media would have had a field day when some of the treasure was found in the waterwheel. I'm surprised there's only two here looking for it. We are going home in two days. If you're concerned about it, talk to Johno, and he can keep an eye on them. I think you're going to get all sorts of people coming here now, and that can only be good for the town.'

*

The two killers had decided to work separately at the start to see what that might bring. The Butcher and the Black Cat were staying just outside London so they wouldn't attract attention to themselves around the small town. It was only a forty-five-minute trip each day back to where they were staying near London.

The Butcher of Boston went to the girls school next to the church, and the Black Cat went to the church. She was a Catholic, but she wouldn't be doing any confessions with the priest; not that day, anyway.

The Butcher of Boston rang the bell at the old convent girls school but there was no response. There were only two nuns there now, waiting for the decision by the Catholic councillors to decide on the future outcome of the girls school.

The Butcher wandered round to the back of the building and found Sister Theresa digging in the vegetable garden.

'Hello,' she said, 'how can I help?'

'I'm here to pick up Calico Jack's treasure.'

'Then you must know where it is, then.'

'No I don't, but I know you do.'

'I'm sorry, you have been misinformed. I don't think anyone knows, and most people here think it's all just rumours.'

'Don't give me that bullshit, and don't think you can hide behind those black clothes. Last chance, lady!'

'I can't tell you what I don't know.'

He grabbed her and cut her face to pieces with his cutthroat razor, and threw her face into the vegetable garden.

The Black Cat was admiring the fascinating old church when a soft, male, biblical sort of voice said, 'Hello, my dear, can I help you?'

No, thank you. I'm just admiring this lovely old church.'

'I can't tell you much about it – I've only been here two weeks myself – but if you go to the town hall and see Dee, she will show you where the journals are of the history of the church.'

'Then I don't suppose you would know much about the treasure that's hidden here somewhere.'

'I gather, talking to the locals, no one seems to know much about it. I think, because it was supposed to have been hidden here hundreds of years ago, people have put it down as a myth and gone on with their lives. Once again, you will find what's known about the so-called treasure in the journals at the town hall.'

'Is the church open at night for quiet prayer?

'Yes, my child. The church never closes.'

'What happened to the old priest who was here?'

'I'm told he was murdered. Why anyone would want to murder a priest, I wouldn't know.'

'Well, he obviously knew or found out something he wasn't supposed to know or see. Why else would they kill a priest?'

*

Sister Claudine found Sister Theresa face down in the vegetable garden, with her face so badly cut to pieces her eyeballs were no longer there and had to be looked for in the garden. Her nose had been completely severed and her mouth had been cut open from ear to ear. The police and coroner arrived and discovered her face had been completely dissected.

Johno said, 'Christ, look at that! What sort of person would inflict that on another human being?'

The coroner said, 'Whoever did this can never be called human. They develop their own twisted, sick mind as they go. There is no doubt they should be put down immediately when caught. There is no chance of rehabilitation with these sick people.'

'Well, it won't be one of our locals. It's someone who's visiting, or visited, with a twisted brain. You can almost pick who they are just by looking at them. They somehow look different from a normal person, but getting enough evidence to convict them is another thing.'

*

Max's phone rang.

'Meet me at the pub,' the voice said.

'What's up, Johno?' Max said.

'Sister Theresa has been murdered, and her face has been cut up real bad. Sister Claudine is on her own now and has been told to lock the old convent up, not to go out for anything and not to open the door unless she knows who they are and can be trusted. If she needs anything, the police will get it for her.'

The Spiders arrived and Johno went over everything.

'Sorry,' they said, 'we are going home tomorrow.'

'Well, I'm sorry also. I have spoken to Harrigan. He said you could stay here for one more week and then you must go back. But it's entirely up to you what you do.'

They had a quiet discussion.

Jane said, 'Okay, you've got your one week. Then, regardless of what happens, we are going home.'

'Jesus,' Lois said, 'why is it we can never go anywhere without a saga? We're all just getting over escaping the claws of death in that awful Venezuelan rainforest. We only came back to get our things.'

*

The Black Cat and the Boston Butcher had been told about the Spiders. There were eight of them, they were old but damned good at what they did. They were dangerous and proficient with most weapons and weren't to be judged lightly because of their age. But it was understood they had gone home, so they wouldn't be an issue. They thought they would have a free hand. The small local police station shouldn't cause much of an issue either.

They were driving back to London when they heard over the car radio that a sister by the name of Theresa had been murdered at the old convent girl's school in Hambleden, and her face had been cut up badly.

The Black Cat was driving the vehicle. She pulled over to the side of the road and said, 'Why would you want to kill a defenceless nun, for Christ's sake? You are a sick, bloody idiot. Now we've got the Marlow police and homicide detectives from London crawling all over Hambleden. Why does The Syndicate persist in giving me brainless mental morons to work with? Not only have I got the authorities cramping my investigation for the treasure, but you have seen fit to kill an innocent nun and cut her up for no reason, except that you're a sadistic prick. There are some rules in what we do.'

She was so angry that she shot him six times and rolled him out into the deep drain on the side of the road into the long grass. Now she could get on with the job at hand. Besides that, she now had the contract money all to herself.

*

'Where is Anne, our direct descendent of Bonny? We haven't seen her yet. Does anyone think that is strange?' said Lois. 'When we go back to the pub tonight, let's ask around.'

The bartender said Anne had gone to a friend's place in London the day before the Spiders had arrived, but she would be back the next day.

*

While the homicide detectives were finishing up their investigation at the old convent girls school, they were being watched by the Black Cat from under the large elm trees growing outside along the stone wall of the church. When they had gone, she decided to check out the graveyard before it got dark, then she would eat at the Stag and Huntsman pub. She flipped the rusty metal gate loop over the top of the gate that held the old wooden picket gates together. The graveyard was split into two sections: the older graves high on the hill, which would now just be gatherings of bones, the more recent graves down closer to the gate where there were quite a few sites with recently turned soil and fresh flowers.

She closed the gate and climbed the slope to the older section of the graveyard. Most of the headstones were worn out from the passage of time, and although broken and damaged from the harsh weather, they had kept their promise and were standing watch over their grave sites. A gentle breeze was clearing the crumpled yellow birch leaves off the concrete slabs and surrounds. As she walked among the graves, she asked herself what she was doing here, and what information she could possibly get from the people under her feet who had been dead for hundreds of years. *There must be something here that will push me in the right direction*, she said to herself.

She saw the steps that went down to the broken door that Hanna and Rosie had gone through into the crypt for a smoke. The Black Cat squeezed herself past the broken door and found herself in a large room with three coffins. She read the inscriptions, but they had nothing to do with why she was here, so she moved on. Although it was still daylight outside, it was dark in the crypt, and she only had a very small keyring torch. She followed the crypt along to the end, studying the steel caskets on their shelves in the wall and reading the inscriptions by the flimsy torch light as she went along.

The last casket near a set of wooden stairs had an inscription done in 2008 that read, "Money and jewellery are the sins of God. RIP forever". The casket latches were undone. She raised the casket lid. It was empty. She leaned over and put her hand in to get a better look with the small torch. A small diamond was in the corner of the casket, left behind by the military when they had taken all the diamonds and treasure out during their inventory of the dead and empty caskets in the crypt.

'Hello there,' she said when she saw the diamond, 'and where have all your little friends gone?'

She took the small diamond and closed the lid of the casket. There was a trapdoor at the top of the stairs, but it was locked, and from where she was, she thought this must lead to the church somewhere. As soon as she got a chance, she would visit the church again.

Chapter Fifty

The Spiders were in the Stag and Huntsman having drinks with Johno, off duty and in his civilian clothes, before they ordered their meal. The Black Cat walked in, got a wine at the bar and sat by herself at a table in the corner.

Max said, 'Who is the blonde dolly?'

Johno said, 'No idea. Never seen her before. With what's been happening lately, I wonder what she's up to. You know, before you Spiders got here, we had a quiet little town. Harrigan told me, while the Spiders are in town, it won't be quiet, but when they've gone, the problems will be gone with them. Jesus, when are you going?'

Lois said, 'Well, Johno, you've got a short memory. You're the one who begged us to stay.'

'Yeah, yeah, and I'm grateful.'

After the meal, he said, 'I'd better go and see who she is, I suppose.'

'Hello,' he said, 'I'm Sergeant John Weir from the local police station. Welcome to our humble town. May I ask what brings you here?'

'Hello,' she said, 'I am Catrina. I'm on a holiday with my

husband. We heard the interesting stories about the pirate's treasure, so we decided to come and see for ourselves. Unfortunately, my husband had to return home for a serious illness in his family. Because of the expense to get here, I decided to stay.'

'Where have you come from?' Johno said.

'We are from New Zealand. I'll stay here a few days out of interest in the pirate's treasure.'

'Well,' Johno said, 'I'll be watching to see how you get on. If you find the treasure and buy the town, I need to be your friend to keep my job.'

She smiled and said, 'I don't think it would come to that, but I'll remember this conversation. May I call you John?'

'Out of uniform, absolutely. In uniform, you, like everyone else here, will call me Sergeant Weir. Nice meeting you, Catrina. Oh, and by the way, where are you staying?'

'Just this side of London. It's only a forty-five-minute drive back if I want to return.'

As she left, she said to herself, *Well, that was a mistake on my part, eating in the same town I'm operating in and running into that bloody cop!*

*

The next day, they were looking forward to seeing Anne again. It was midday, confirmed by the high-pitched whistle that went off, and given it was only about a ninety-minute drive from London, if that's where she really was, they expected her back by now. When it came time for the evening meal, Anne had still not arrived. The other worry was that nobody knew exactly where she was going or who she had been seeing, not even her closest friends. They only knew she had gone to London to stay with a friend, and she was due back that day.

So, where was she, and who killed Sister Theresa? Were they connected or not? Max didn't think so.

*

The Black Cat had found the trapdoor in the church. She knew where it went, that a part of the treasure had been removed from the casket and the main bulk of it was still somewhere in this town, to be discovered.

Sergeant Weir had tasked a constable to tail and watch this so-called Catrina, at the end of his shift to report on her activities and hand over to the oncoming shift. The Black Cat was a professional and she soon realised she kept seeing the same bobby wherever she went. She was not going to be free to do what she wanted with him on his pushbike everywhere she went. She pulled her car over and watched him peddle past and turn down a side country lane. There was no one to be seen, so she pulled out from the curb, turned the corner, sped up and ran right over the top of him, killing him instantly. The car had minor scratch marks from the pushbike. She drove it back to London and returned it, moving on to another hire car company and hiring a Volkswagen hatchback. She stayed in London that night and drove back to Hambleden the next morning.

The whole town was shocked and angry that one of their own had been the victim of a hit-and-run. Inspectors from London and Scotland Yard were examining every car that was registered in the town, along with their driver's address in the town, and any other vehicle that happened to be there, including the Black Cat's car.

*

Anne had finally arrived back from London, or so she said. She said she didn't have anyone to answer to, so she'd stayed another day. The Black Cat was watching the crowd of people in the street. Apart from the old lady, they looked like a government black ops team, but they were far too old; however, there was something about them that spelt danger. She thought, *The Spiders are not supposed to be here but you can tell by the way these people carry themselves, I'm willing to bet they are the Spiders, all right. What are they doing back here? Jesus, they're worse than the police!*

She stopped a woman in the street and asked her who the old lady was.

'I might know her, but I would be embarrassed if it wasn't who I think is.'

The woman said, 'That's Anne Campbell, one of the locals.'

'Thank you. I'm glad I asked.'

When she had been in the graveyard and the crypt, she had seen several Campbell graves from the 1700s, the same era as Calico Jack and his hidden treasure, and she wondered how much this old lady knew. Her relatives certainly had lived here during the days Calico Jack was supposed to have hidden his treasure there, and she wondered if this woman had any connection to the treasure she was looking for, or if there had been information passed down through the family over time.

Anne was coming out of the butcher shop when she was approached by the Black Cat.

'Hello, Mrs Campbell, my name is Catrina. Sergeant Weir said if I wanted to know about the rumoured treasure, I should talk to you. Would you be free tonight for a while to have a talk? I could meet you at the church, if you like.'

Anne said, 'Look, I don't know any more than most of the locals know, but I'm happy to tell you what I know.'

The Black Cat said, 'Would 7 pm be all right?'

'Yes, that's fine. I live by myself, so I have plenty of time.'

The Black Cat got to the church early and found the trapdoor to the crypt in case she needed it. Anne arrived and they sat in the pews at the front of the church.

The Black Cat said, 'You talk, I'll just listen.'

Anne told the Black Cat about the wrong information passed down through the family, the coins found in the paddles of the flour mill's waterwheel, and the diamonds, jewellery and money found by the Spiders in the casket in the crypt that the government now had. Calico Jack might never have even been there at all, never mind coming back. The pirate, Calico Jack, had been real all right, but the rest of the story might just be rumours.

'Mind you,' Anne said, 'you must ask yourself if all that is rumour, where did the loot come from in the casket? Is there something else going on here that no one knows about? The treasure in the casket that was found had something to do with a nun from the girl's school. She murdered another nun and fled, so where did she get the diamonds from? The whole town of Hambleden now is just one big mystery, complicated now with two murders. And holy mother of Jesus, that a sick person would want to kill and cut up an innocent nun just begs belief. I have lived eighty-two years on this planet and have never seen anything so cold and ruthless.'

'Well, all that may be so, but what about the rumours of Anne Bonny coming back here?'

'I suppose it all balances on whether Calico Jack came back. I doubt that Bonny would have come back here by herself, and if Calico had come back to England, what was the attraction here at Hambleden? I don't believe any of it. So, forget all the rumours of Calico Jack. There really are only two questions, aren't there –where did the money and diamonds come from, and how did the nun get hold of them to hide in the casket?'

Anne went to the cottage later that night to see the Spiders, unaware that she had been followed. She told them that this woman named Catrina wanted to know all about Bonny, and the information she had about the deceased Campbell family could only have been obtained from the inscriptions on the coffins in the crypt.

'I think this woman is very dangerous.'

They said they would get her checked out. Although Catrina wouldn't be her real name, and neither would her passport, they would take a trip to London to check on her when she left that day.

The Black Cat saw them come to the door, and now she knew who they were.

Chapter Fifty-One

Sister Claudine was on her own in the old convent school now, so she could come and go as she pleased through the secret door in the large wardrobe in the Mother Superior's bedroom. It was a shame that she had had to kill the Mother Superior, who knew nothing about the secret door, but she had seen Claudine coming out of the wardrobe one night, so Claudine had no choice.

The door led to a set of stairs running down to a large room where Sister Claudine kept the diamonds and other treasures she had stolen. There were three tunnels: one led to the crypt, another to the church and one came out under the newly built bench seat where Anne had said some of the treasure was buried. The treasure was no longer under the seat, and it turned out to be only a small amount, after all. It had been taken from under the seat from the tunnel by "Sister Ignatius", that is, Zilla, and kept in the casket in the crypt. Sister Claudine had been stealing the diamonds from the African mining company owned by Rosanna's parents. Zilla and Claudine had shared an agreement of silence of each other's activities, although it had cost Claudine some of her diamonds. Anyone who looked like they were getting too close to what they were doing was disposed of, including the two nuns and the Mother Superior.

Sister Claudine was sick of seeing people live a lavish lifestyle while she had no possessions of her own, no nice clothes, and no chance to show them off if even she'd had them. The diamonds she was stealing were to go to a client in Marlow. She had a silent partner, a seaman on the boat who delivered the diamonds to her. She would meet him in the graveyard at night, go down in the crypt, carefully unwrap the diamonds, give him one stone, tip the rest into her stocking, fill the box with plastic beads and carefully rewrap the diamond package the way it had been and the seaman would take the parcel back to the boat for delivery. The diamond thefts had been investigated many times with no answer to where they were going. That's why Joran had come to Hambleden, to solve the diamond thefts when he was murdered by Zilla.

*

The Black Cat thought she was wasting her time. There was probably no more treasure to be found, if there had been any in the first place. The Syndicate had told her to keep a lookout for the diamonds that seemed to vanish when they got to Hambleden. After talking to Anne, she was inclined to agree with her logic about the treasure, so her priority would now be the diamonds. The Syndicate would not allow her to return with nothing.

*

The Spiders decided to split up. Max and Jane would tail Catrina back to London, Joe and Lois would visit Sister Claudine to see what she might know but hadn't revealed yet and Bruce and Sue would revisit the Bonny grave in case they had missed something when they were last there. Joe and Lois didn't need transport, but Bruce and Sue did, so they went with Max and Jane to hire a small car in London.

Catrina was staying in what looked from the outside to be a small bedsitter in Bexley, a suburb on the outskirts of London. They wrote down the address and the number plate of the car. They used their ASIS police credentials to locate the car hire company and paid them a visit. The date she had hired the car was the same day the bobby had been killed on his bicycle. They also knew she had had a car before the one she had now. There was only one other car hirer in this area, so they paid him a visit as well. The car she had hired from this place had been returned the same day as the hit-and-run. The car was a Volkswagen Beetle and was still in the yard and had not been hired out since it was returned. When they examined it, they found slight damage to the front of the vehicle with what looked like traces of black paint from the bicycle. They rang Johno to set the wheels in motion to have forensic checks for residue of the black police push bike. Now they would have to wait for the results, but they were positive that it was the car that had killed the police officer.

*

Bruce and Sue were on their way across the field to the grave site of Anne Bonny.

Sue said, 'Is that someone at the gravesite?'

'Certainly looks like it,' said Bruce.

When they arrived, there was a small round container set into the middle of the sunken grave, which was now full of fresh flowers, but where was the person they had seen there five minutes ago? The farmer who had shot Three Fingers lived nearby. His house was surrounded by a four-foot hedge and was too far away for anyone to have gone there and not been seen. They studied the grave and saw nothing abnormal. They walked around the big tree and looked up into it. They gave up and went back to town.

*

Joe and Lois rang the bell at the big oak door of the convent.

Joe said, 'We need to find a back door somewhere and unlock it so we can get back in tonight.'

The small square in the front door slid open.

Sister Claudine said, 'Hello there, I thought you people had gone back to Australia.'

Lois said, 'We came back for our belongings, and now we are helping with an investigation of a murder and theft, but we will be going home in a couple of days.'

'So, how can I help you?'

'We need to come in and look around for anything that might help us with the murder of Sister Theresa, and we need to see her room. If you're not happy, I can ring Sergeant Weir for you to talk to, if you wish. But one way or another, we will be coming in to check,' said Joe.

'There's no need to do that.'

She knew if the police came, they would search everywhere. This was, she thought, just a quick search, and they would be gone. She let them in.

As they walked through the big hall, Lois said, 'What a wonderfully interesting place! I bet it could tell some chilling stories of the past.'

Sister Claudine took them to Sister Theresa's room. Lois said to herself, *My God, look how they make these women live!* There was a small single wire and tubular bed with a thin mattress, a small dressing table with three drawers with a bible resting on top and a single door metal locker for the few clothes they were permitted. There was no mirror or anything that suggested that this was a woman's room. There was nothing to see in Sister Theresa's room.

'We need to know that you are safe, so we have been asked to check all the doors for your security while we are here,' Joe said. 'We know you would have them all locked, but the police need to make sure they are. When we put our tag on the door, it means they have been security checked and they're not to be touched. We won't put a tag on the front door. You need to have somewhere to be able to come and go, if you wish.'

Lois looked at Joe in amazement. He smiled and pulled from his pocket small plastic table number cards that he had taken from the pub. As they went around the doors, he checked they were locked and jammed a card in the door. When they got to the door he wanted, he checked it was locked while the nun watched, and when Lois pointed to something and the nun looked away, Joe unlocked the door.

The Spiders got together at the pub to discuss what they each had done that day. Bruce and Sue told everyone about the disappearance of someone at Bonny's grave, and they talked about the time it had happened at the graveyard.

People just can't vanish into thin air, so that was food for thought. Max and Jane said they were now just waiting on the forensic report for Catrina's car, but they were sure this woman had been the driver of the car that had killed the police officer. Joe and Lois told them they had left a back door unlocked at the convent, and they intended to go back to have a good look at night. However, they decided now that was too risky. They would ask Johno to drive her to the police station to make a written statement. While she was gone, they could go in through the back door and check the place out properly.

Joe and Lois weren't convinced that Sister Claudine was the mild-mannered nun she would have everyone believe she was.

Chapter Fifty-Two

The only person they hadn't spoken to yet was the farmer who had shot the goon called Three Fingers. So, they headed on out there. The farm was about ninety metres from Bonny's grave and was surrounded by a well-cared-for high cypress hedge. An archway had been cut into the hedge where the white picket gate acknowledged their arrival with a squeak and a groan as they opened it. A slight breeze ruffled their hair and carried the smell of fresh cow manure to their nostrils, adding its fragrance to the farm's day-to-day activities. The rustic farmhouse spoke of days gone by, the days of horse-drawn carts and ploughs, now all sitting in a world that had advanced beyond its time. There was a freshly ploughed field down one side of the house and a harvested field next to it with a large haystack in the middle of the field. There were a couple of poddy calves being fed fresh cow's milk from a bucket by the farmer down the side of the house yard.

Auntie Sue said, 'Why are they called poddy calves?'

Max said, 'Poddy calves are orphaned calves. Their mother could be dead, or she has rejected the calf. They can be very difficult to rear.'

Max knew from his own time that being on a farm could

be both rewarding and heartbreaking, and was not for the faint-hearted. It required patience and commitment. Calves had many considerations for rearing, due to the rumen in the stomach that helps digest solids like lucerne, garden plants and flowers. Calves' rumen would not be formed enough to help digest the solids, so these types of food needed to be given carefully and in small portions at the correct time of rearing.

Max said, 'If you haven't stood in green, soft and runny smelly calf shit yet, you haven't lived.'

The farmer saw them as he was coming along the wooden veranda past an old cane rocking chair, dodging the sticky fly tape hanging from the veranda's rafters, followed by his loyal border collie bobbing along behind him.

He said, 'I have seen you here with Anne, haven't I?'

'Yes, they said.

'Well, you must be all right if she brought you here to the grave.'

They introduced themselves. His name was Cedric and he lived here alone with fifty milking cows, a hundred and twenty sheep, fifty acres of wheat and two fields of lucerne, which kept him busy from dawn till dusk.

'So, how can I help you?'

They showed him their credentials and said, 'We just need to go over the shooting when Anne was tied up at the grave.'

'Darndest thing. I came out early to get the cows in for milking and there she was, all tied up at the grave site. She said a man and a woman were trying to get information about Bonny and the treasure. They didn't believe what she'd told them, so they tied her up and left her there all night. I untied her and we saw them coming back through the field. They both had guns. I always take my rifle to get the cows in, because I sometimes see a fox. Anne hid behind the blackberry bushes, and I shot the bastard. The woman crawled away in the long grass, then I heard a car start up and leave. Anne comes here at least once a week to replace the flowers on the grave. I help by letting the sheep graze around the gravesite to keep the grass down. And it gives the dead a chance to be surrounded by life, with the sheep grazing and chewing their cud, and the birth of lambs in springtime, fulfilling the promise of new life. The sheep gives a cold and lonely gravesite a warm and welcoming feeling.'

Max said, 'Does anyone else ever come to see the grave?'

'If they do, I have never seen anyone. Anne is the only one I have seen here.'

Jane said, 'Do you know who it is who's buried there?'

'I believe it is Anne's great-great-grandmother. This farm was my parents' farm and I was born here. I can remember the grave here under the trees from when I was a small boy. The grave would have been there long before this farm was, and long before my parents were born, so it's certainly earned its right to be there, wouldn't you say?'

'We can't argue with that,' Jane said. 'Well, thanks for giving us your time. You obviously need every minute of it.'

'What did you say your surname was?' said Max.

'I didn't say, and you didn't ask, but since you have, it's Cedric Campbell.'

They said thanks and left.

'Christ,' said Jane, 'did you hear that? He is a Campbell. In a little village like this, and born here, he and his parents would have to be related to Anne, wouldn't they? So, why didn't he say something when we were talking about the grave, and why hasn't Anne mentioned it? Remember, some time ago, Lois and I said we didn't think Anne was telling us everything? That's just been proven correct.'

*

The company where the Black Cat had hired the second car from thought they were doing the right thing and rang her about the people asking questions about her. She knew it was only a matter of time before they knew who had run over the police officer. She needed to work fast from now on and somehow stay undercover. She decided to pay the convent girls school a visit.

*

Sergeant Weir rang the bell at the big oak doors and the square panel slid open.

Sister Claudine said, 'Is everything all right?'

'Yes, but you need to come back with me to the station to make a written statement and sign it.'

'But I've already made a statement.'

'Yes I know you have, but we need a *written* statement.'

'All right, I'll be with you in a moment.'

*

Joe and Lois came in through the back door they had left unlocked on their last visit.

'That's funny,' Joe said. 'The number card I jammed in the door should have fallen on the floor when we opened it and that would have told us no one had opened this door. But now we've opened it, the card is across the floor. See, it's way over there. We specifically told Sister Claudine the doors were not to be touched.'

There were corridors, stairs and rooms everywhere. Although it was daylight, inside the convent there was an eerie feeling. It reminded Lois of the quote, "You can't have a home without love, as it just becomes a house". They didn't feel any love or warmth here, like the flowers growing in the courtyard garden that needed warmth to grow and share their colourful images. The only image being shared here was untold stories of monsters and boogeymen, sinister acts and children scared witless. The big windows up high were like strange eyes looking in, doing their best to soften and warm this cold, hard environment.

Joe said, 'This place has no purpose if there was no love given by its occupants.'

Lois said, 'I'm glad we're not doing this in the dark.'

They heard the whizzing sound of the bullet before they heard the pop of the silencer as the bullet grazed Joe's ear and splintered the wooden door frame behind him.

Lois said, 'Someone is up there with a gun.'

'No shit, Sherlock!' said Joe, holding his bleeding ear.

There were two more shots from the room on the left. Further up the passageway, they saw the red tracer rounds searching for their target. The Black Cat had found the unlocked back door and had been inside the convent for some time, arriving just as Sister Claudine had left with the police, which probably saved her life. The Black Cat had been there long enough to find what she had come for. Claudine had left the secret door in the wardrobe slightly open, providing an escape route for her, and now it was time to leave as she knew the intruders were the Spiders.

There had been no shooting for some time. The hairy spider and his female mate (Joe and Lois) crept along the passageway towards the room with a sign on the door that read, "Mother Superior. Please knock before entering". The shots had come from this room. There was still no movement from inside, so they cautiously entered to find it empty.

Joe said, 'This is just crazy. People at a gravesite one minute and gone the next, and now another disappearing act. Maybe whoever it was has come out the door when we weren't looking, and they're still in here somewhere.'

'Well, if that's the case, why aren't they still trying to kill us?' Lois said, 'The place is so big I don't think we have time to check every nook and cranny before Claudine comes back, and I wouldn't mind getting out of here.'

*

The Black Cat found the diamonds in the room down in the tunnels to the church and the crypt. She had been in the crypt before, so she knew her way around. She continued on until she reached the broken door to the graveyard. She chose an old grave with these words on the headstone: "The love you gave us was worth diamonds. RIP, my sweet lady." She placed the diamonds in the old flower container, took some old, dried flowers stems from other graves and stuffed them into the container to make sure the diamonds were covered, and the container looked normal and hadn't been disturbed.

Now she needed somewhere to hide till dark.

Chapter Fifty-Three

The forensic results confirmed that the car driven by the Black Cat had been the car that had killed the police officer on the pushbike, so now the hunt was on. The police and Spiders had the description of her car, and if it was in the small town, it wouldn't take long to find it. It didn't, but she wasn't in it.

'That means,' Max said, 'she is here somewhere on foot.'

The police and the Spiders split up. Bruce and Sue went to the convent girls school, Joe and Lois to the graveyard and Max and Jane to the crypt via the church. The police used their cars to cover the town and surrounding areas.

Sister Claudine had now been returned to the convent.

It didn't take Joe and Lois long to search the graveyard, so they went into the crypt through the broken door in the graveyard.

'This place unnerves me,' said Lois, 'so hurry up so we can get out of here.'

Lois was getting very concerned with all these trips to the graveyard, as she had been told by several of the town people that if a ghost takes a liking to you, they will follow you home, male or female as the case may be.

Joe said, 'Well, that won't happen to me, Lois. I've outsmarted them by walking out of the graveyard backwards each time we've been here.'

Lois said, 'Well, thanks for telling me. I suppose it's too late for me to do that now.'

'How many times have you been here, Lois?'

'Three times here and twice at the one in the meadow.'

'Okay, go down to the graveyard gate and come in and out backwards five times.'

As she did so, Joe sat on the seat outside the gate and watched as tears of happiness ran down his leg.

Max and Jane were coming through the trapdoor from the church into the crypt as Bruce and Sue were ringing the bell at the majestic oak doors. There was no answer, so they walked around the building searching for the door that Joe and Lois had left open. They found the unlocked door that Joe and Lois had gone through, calling out, 'Is anyone there?' As they climbed the narrow stairs, they saw the tracer round too late, and Bruce was hit in the pelvis.

Sue said, 'Jesus, Bruce, how many times do you want to be shot? It's not a competition.'

Sue returned the fire.

Bruce said, 'If you manage to hit them, I'll bet its somewhere out of the ordinary.'

She took off her blouse and packed Bruce's wound. She stayed with him for a while to make sure he was all right.

'Stay there and I'll get help.'

'Where would you think I'd be going, Sue?'

The other four Spiders met in the crypt, coming in from each end. Just as they were about to say, 'There's nobody here', Lois was hit in the right breast, and down she went.

'I'm okay. Just keep going. I've no doubt I'll still be here when you get back, one way or the other.'

There were two tunnels that hadn't been discovered before. Max and Jane took one and Joe took the other.

Max said, 'This one doesn't look too long, and there's a door I can see at the other end.'

They went through the door into a large two-door wardrobe and came out in the Mother Superior's room.

'Jesus,' Jane said, 'talk about the house of horrors, mirrors and surprises.'

Lying on the floor was Sister Claudine, who had been shot. She had lost a lot of blood and was barely alive. She beckoned Jane to kneel next to her.

She whispered, 'The diamonds are gone. That woman took them.'

Her eyes closed, and she was dead. They heard voices, and they knew Bruce and Sue were coming to the convent and would be inside somewhere. They carefully turned the corner and looked up the stairs to find Bruce and Sue lying on the stairs halfway up, and they realised Bruce had been hit. They rang the police and and ambulance. Max went back through the wardrobe to the crypt to tell Lois an ambulance was on the way.

Lois said, 'Joe went down that tunnel over there.'

Max said, 'Will you be all right?'

'Yes. Just go.'

This tunnel led to the trapdoor into the church which had been lifted and open. When Joe stuck his head up, he was nicked in the same ear, bleeding again.

'Shit!' he said. 'Thankfully, she's about as good as Sue with a gun.'

Max arrived behind Joe, who said, 'She will never let us up through here. I'll keep her busy with a shot every now and then, and you hurry back and come into the church from the front.'

Max went back through the graveyard and crept into the church from the front door through the narthex and crawled along the rows of pews toward the sanctuary where the priest normally stands, but in this case, where the Black Cat was firing from. Max knew once he left the cover of the pews he would be shot, so he needed a diversion of some sort.

He rang Sergeant Weir and whispered, 'Don't ask, I can't talk, but as quickly as you can, send someone to ring the church bells. And I mean, right now!'

Someone must have been close by. It wasn't long before the deafening bells rang out. The Black Cat stuck her head up and Max shot her. When he got to her, she smiled at him and said, 'Diamonds in the graveyard, hidden from all.'

He smiled back and said, 'Spider, spider on the wall, how is it you never fall?'

She looked at him, confused, and was dead.

Chapter Fifty-Four

Bruce and Lois were now out of hospital, and the police had failed to find the diamonds in the graveyard.

'I can't believe I'm saying this, but we need your help and brains to find these diamonds,' said Johno.

Now the Spiders were involved, the hunt would begin again. They knew these diamonds were real and were in the graveyard somewhere. The Spiders and the police, for the second time now, had the task of scouring the graveyard for the diamonds. Jane and Lois both agreed the woman wouldn't just dump the diamonds in any old grave. There would have to be a rhyme and reason to her decision.

Lois said, 'Look at these pommy cops, will you, Jane? They wouldn't find a horse in a barn till it bit them on the arse.'

The police were working the newer area and the Spiders were up the hill in the old area. The police were wandering around with no purpose or idea what they supposed to be doing.

Jane and Lois went among the police and said, 'Come over here, the lot of you. You need to read the headstone for any clues, not just walk around with hands in pocket, playing with the family jewels. Don't ask me what you're looking specifically, for I don't know, but you will know when you read it, I'll bet. It will have something to do with bloody diamonds ... You do know that's what we are all looking for, don't you?'

They looked at Jane and Lois, grinning, and said, 'Yes, Ma'am!'

'So, get on with it then,' Lois said, smiling back at them.

Instead of just wandering around with their hands in their pockets, they were tasked with reading every headstone.

As they went, she called out, 'Let's face it, gentleman, we're not asking you to read all the headstones at the London cemetery, are we? So, look like you're enjoying yourself and go find the diamonds.'

They found several that got them excited. The first one said, "Diamonds are forever, but not so human life." They were convinced this was the grave, and when it wasn't, they were worried they had the wrong slant on their thinking. But they kept at it.

A police officer called out, "Over here, over here!"

They all hurried over and read the inscription: "They said you were a kind and gentle soul, but to me you were just a diamond in the rough. Your passing has broken my heart. Time to fly, my pigeon."

They searched everywhere, but no luck. They were about to try another idea when Sue called out.

'What about this one? "The love you gave us was worth diamonds. RIP, my sweet lady".'

And there in the old metal tin that held the flowers and stems of time were the diamonds.

'Well,' Johno said, 'you people are as good as they say you

are, so hurry up and get on the plane home. I want a normal life again.'

They said, 'Oh, we will, but we have one more puzzle to unravel.'

*

They were having their usual meal in the pub with Johno, who said, 'I'll miss you lot when you go, but don't come back. I'll come to see you in Australia.'

Max said, 'By the way, did you ever work out why somebody was at the cottage while we were away, but didn't steal anything?'

'No, but my men said someone had been digging in the vegetable garden. Must have been stealing the vegetables.'

They all looked at each other in shock.

'So, why were they *inside* the cottage? Doesn't make any sense,' said Sue.

'Be that as it may,' said Johno, 'there was nothing stolen, maybe a spud and a carrot, so case closed.'

'Jesus, you will never make a Spider,' they said.

'Right,' said Lois, 'last question – how much do you know about Cedric Campbell?'

Johno said, 'He runs a family farm about nine kilometres from here, a hardworking man who keeps to himself, probably due to every hour it takes to run the farm.'

'Do you know if he is related to Anne Campbell?'

Lois now needed to be very careful where all this went. The disclosure they had signed had a lot to do with the name Campbell and the treasure.

Johno said, 'I've never given it much thought. People here,

275

Lois, mind their own business and don't get involved in others affairs, if you get my drift. And as long as they don't break the law, that's fine by me.'

Lois had just been told to leave it alone and it was none of anyone's business, including hers, but there were some things that still didn't add up. The fact that the name Campbell had Johno "throwing his toys out of the cot" also meant they had poked a bear, hit a nerve, and that the Bonny and Ryan Campbell story was by no means finished. Why hadn't Anne and Cedric told them they were cousins? The Spiders had all signed the non-disclosure form, so why were secrets being kept from them?

It was coming on dusk, but they decided to go back to the farm and the grave anyway. Lois poked her tongue out at Johno as they left. They went via the cottage for torches and their weapons. As they were getting through the wire fence into the meadow where the farm was, what there was of the day's mild sun had almost reached the tree line in the distance, and would soon nestle among the trees, giving the canopy an orange glow, reminding the birds it was time to find their way home. They had all walked through this meadow on other occasions when visiting the grave or the farm, but somehow today seemed different, as if they had been accepted as friends of the meadow and the critters in it, as if they all knew the Spiders were going home tomorrow and were saying goodbye. The shadows of the trees, like long thin fingers, were reaching out across the meadow, killing the daylight around them as the fingers grew longer and longer. Little critters and insects scurried along in front of them as they walked towards the grave and the farm.

By the time the grave was visible, the transformation of day into night had drenched them in darkness. A flimsy looking pale moon was doing its best to light things up, turning objects into all sorts of weird shapes. As they moved slowly and quietly around the grave, not wanting to offend the dead, anyone watching from a distance would have seen black figures wandering in the dark around a grave like ghosts that had come out for a stroll.

Max went over to the old stump and said, 'Why doesn't the grass grow here?'

He leaned on the stump and it moved. The underneath of the stump was on small rollers and easy to move. They gently moved it and there was a trapdoor. They quietly opened it and heard voices from somewhere below. There must have been a gush of cold air that went down the stairs.

A familiar voice said, 'Come on down, now that you're here.'

They went down, and sitting there were Cedric, Anne and Johno, of all people.

'We have been waiting for you,' Johno said. 'We knew you were coming, and we knew how smart people like you are and that it wouldn't take you long to work it all out.'

Anne said, 'Sit down and I'll explain. The farm was established three generations ago by the Campbells and passed down to Cedric's parents, my auntie and uncle, who died some time ago. So, it's now Cedric's farm. When the Campbells knew the Second World War was coming, they dug and reinforced this bomb shelter that Cedric and I played in as children. The trapdoor and stump are locked and chained when we're not here, which is most of the time. The stump will be removed and the trapdoor concreted over and filled in, now that we know there are other honest people who now know this location, to protect it from being found until the right time comes to use its value. My parents and Cedric's parents knew for many years exactly where the main part of the treasure was hidden. They also knew there were dribs and drabs of it in several places. Over the past fifty years, there have been more and more people with sophisticated equipment coming to look for it. We were concerned that it would eventually fall into the wrong hands, so Cedric and I confided in Sergeant Weir to help recover the treasure and to hide and protect its location. He has signed the same non-disclosure papers as you to ensure in the end the treasure goes to serve the right people.'

'Well,' said Max, 'you'd better be ready to find a trustworthy source that's a lot younger than those of us sitting here. Somewhere in the next ten years, none of the Spiders will be alive.'

She said, 'That will be a very careful and important decision for you all to make on our behalf.'

The bomb shelter had two rooms. One presumably would have been set up as the bedroom and the one they were sitting in for cooking, reading and so on. The treasure was stashed in what would have been the bedroom.

What a sight! Lois and Jane said they couldn't take their eyes of it – diamonds, rubies, coins of all sorts of shapes and sizes, and on a table by itself the golden eagle, and it was solid gold. Sure enough, on the bottom was the words: "The bearer will witness nor suffer no pain, but this eagle must be shared again and again."

The air to the bomb shelter came in through what looked like a container full of flowers in the middle of the makeshift grave which had been put there as a decoy when Bonny had died all those years ago. It didn't have Bonny's name on it but the name Campbell was enough for people to eventually want to dig it up, looking for the treasure. Whenever Anne came to visit her cousin Cedric, she always put flowers in the tin that actually provided air to the bomb shelter on the old makeshift grave site.

Down in the valley, in among the thick rows of windbreak cypress trees among a mat of cones, was a small wooden cross that simply said "Bonny".

Epilogue

The Spiders, separately as husbands and wives, continued their friendship with quite a few of the girls' parents. Max and Jane went to France to Rosie's place and Hanna's in Queensland. Zoe and Molly both lived in Rome, and Max and Jane would be going there next year. The other Spiders had also been invited to various families overseas.

The younger Spiders were now pushing eighty and Max was sneaking up on ninety. With the exception of Joe and Lois, who lived at Lakes Entrance, an eight-hundred-kilometre round trip, four times a year to Fairview was now difficult for the Spiders. They only did June and December now. Those weekend stays twice a year had become important, and precious. They would never forget the dangerous times and good times they had while Bruce was there. They just take out their hearing aids and nod. The girls had, once again, been taken to a private shooting range, where they shot part of the female instructor's ear off.

Her name was Judith Flitcroft, who said, 'There's no bloody hope. Just let the ladies retire!'

They all raised the glasses and said, 'Here's to the Spiders!'

Other books by this author

Hardly a Challenge,
Sid Harta,
Melbourne, 2024,
ISBN 978-1-92295-8860

Spiders of Spy,
Sid Harta,
Melbourne, 2025,
ISBN 978-1-92295-8921